night visits

Ron Butlin

F/1037709

Library of Congress Catalog Card Number: 2003105254

A complete catalogue record for this book can
be obtained from the British Library on request.

The right of Ron Butlin to be identified as the author
of this work has been asserted by him in accordance with
the Copyright, Designs and Patents Act 1988.

First published in 1997 by Scottish Cultural Press

First published by Serpent's Tail in 2003
4 Blackstock Mews, London N4 2BT
website: www.serpentstail.com

This edition is published in association
with blackacebooks.com

Typeset by Volume!
Printed by Mackays of Chatham, plc

10 9 8 7 6 5 4 3 2 1

This book is for Irvine Welsh, Nick Royle, Tom Pow, Hunter Steele, Andrew Greig, Roger Quin, my mother-in-law Dora Staub, my sister Pam Thomson and, of course, my wife Regi – with heartfelt thanks for all their support.

Acknowledgements

I am most grateful to the Scottish Arts Council for a Writer's Bursary which allowed me time to complete this novel. Parts of *Night Visits* have been published as work-in-progress in *New Writing Scotland*, *Edinburgh Review* and broadcast on BBC Radio 4.

Prologue

A few seconds before he died Malcolm's father raised his head from the pillow to look out at the falling snow. Loose flakes were being blown into the top corner of the window, flattening there until one by one they stuck to the glass. There was no sky any more, and no village. Soon the garden itself would disappear.

Three months back he would have managed to the burn; then only to Robson's field. Then the few yards to the start of the low road, with his stick testing the ground and Margaret helping. When he was a child the world had grown bigger every day. Now it was shrinking on every side towards him at dead centre.

He'd been dreaming about that small boat, the tiny metal yacht his father had made for him more than forty years ago. On the wall directly opposite there was a picture of swans flying over a stretch of river. He had dreamt of being on the yacht and drifting easily downstream. By now he knew the landscape by heart. He could close his eyes again and hear the swans' wings beating loudly above him. Loud and steady for a moment, then more and more faint as they passed into the distance, trailing silence after them.

He was never to see them disappear. Nor the trees, the line of low hills or the river itself. At the end only the small yacht remained, having come to rest in the palm of his hand.

I

Evening

1

For the few weeks before his tenth birthday Malcolm saw the world only through his reflection's eyes.

One evening he'd been watching the first snowfall of the winter while *click-click-clicking* his fingers to the new chartbuster straight in at number eight. Usually at this time he would have been looking out the window for the builder's van that brought his dad home. Their meal in the oven to keep hot, he and his mum would have waited and, except for each *flick* as she turned over a page of her magazine, nothing would have happened. He'd have stared and stared into the darkness until finally the van came roaring up the hill, its lights sweeping the village cross where it braked to a stop just long enough for his dad to jump out, slamming the door behind him. At once he'd have turned and rushed out of the kitchen to be at the gate to meet him.

But now, with his dad ill in bed, everything in the house happened differently.

The snow was getting heavier. He couldn't see Stuart's Hill any more and Robson's Farm had started drifting in and out of sight. Swaying, almost, as the snow around it held and fell with each sudden gust of wind.

'Close the curtains, please, Malcolm.'

Click-click-clicking his fingers louder he pretended not to hear.

'Dreaming, are you?' His mother laughed, then came across to the window. She gave the curtains a quick tug and half the village was gone. In the next-door cottage, with its porch light a steadiness between the separate flakes, Sonny was probably playing with the new Gameboy he'd been given. Maybe Malcolm's dad would recover in time to give him one for his birthday? Or maybe he could get his mum to drop a big hint the next time she was on the phone to Aunt Fiona, to save her buying him a book again or another jersey.

His mother had closed the other side, then straightened the curtains where they met. That was that: the night shut out. Like giving up all hope until tomorrow that his dad would get any better.

'We'll be eating soon. Hands washed?'

He nodded. A double finger-click to hurry the record on, he wanted to sing along with the DJ's jingle if it ever came. Jingles were the best part: short and loud. Just like himself, his mother was always saying. She had started laying the table.

'Give's a hand, Malcolm. There's a good boy.'

He pulled open the drawer of the sideboard where the forks and knives lay neatly, each piece in its correct compartment, with the napkins folded on one side.

'Your dad and all, mind.'

'Is he getting up?'

Even after being in his bed for weeks his dad still seemed to be getting older-looking and sweatier every day, and he coughed all the time. Above the sideboard was an oval mirror that showed the room behind him, with his mother putting the cups and plates silently on the table. If he could go into the mirror would it be completely silent, like when he dived into the swimming pool?

In there everything was exactly the same but when he leant closer, the glass was turned into soap water colours or a rainbow along its edge. When he stepped back the colours became clear again. He stared straight into the eyes looking back at him. What would it feel like actually *being* his reflection? The same as looking into the room through a window, maybe?

He waved a fork, and his reflection was already waving it back. He laughed, stuck out his tongue.

'Come along, Malcolm. The tea's nearly ready. Doctor Marshall told your dad he should try getting up for his meals.'

He turned away from the mirror and in a sudden rush made two low–altitude bombing raids on the table:

'Forks away!' followed by 'Knives away!'

Crouching to remain unseen by the enemy, he crept from cover to position the UN plane drops exactly on target: three places all set, the sauce-bottle and salt standing in the centre. Now for the moment he never liked: going into his dad's room.

'I'll call him, will I?'

'You'll go in and tell him properly. If he's not up to it yet, say I'll bring him his dinner on a tray, same as usual.'

He'd better hurry. The record was nearly ending and he didn't want to miss the jingle. Anyway, what was wrong with giving him a shout? His dad wasn't deaf, just ill. Having crossed the small lobby, he paused outside the door. Behind him the record was swinging into the last chorus. He'd have to be quick. Because of the cold the window was never opened, so his dad's room always stank of clothes-smell. And bed-smell and illness-smell. A pity there was no letter-box to shout through.

He knocked. But not too loud, in case his mother heard and would know he'd not gone in as he'd been told. He waited, then bent down to the keyhole and whispered loudly:

'Dad, Dad!'

A faint light showed, so he must be awake. One last try at knocking, one last whisper:

'Dad!'

But it was no good.

He touched the door-handle as lightly as possible. Its metal surface felt greasy and disgusting, making him shiver all over. He turned it quickly and gave the door a push.

Half open.

The loud *tick-tick-tick* of the wind-up alarm clock; the sickly yellow of the bed light; the heavy furniture that filled the rest of the room like darkness. And the smell. Getting worse by the second. It was like sticking his head under water, and into very dirty water at that.

Before going in he leant back into the corridor to take a deep breath, then pushed the door open wide:

'Dad, your tea's ready.'

His father was sitting up in bed looking directly at him as if he'd known he was going to enter the room exactly at that moment. His hands rested on the covers and, as usual, he was wearing his pyjamas with a vest on underneath. The grey stained vest he never seemed to change. When he came through for tea he'd probably just put on a pullover and trousers on top.

The rest of his message delivered, Malcolm stood waiting. Then he repeated it:

'If you want, Mum said she'd bring your dinner through. Okay?'

Had his dad gone deaf suddenly? Or dumb? Well, he couldn't hold his breath any longer. A swallow of the underwater stink, then he went further into the room. He reached out and tapped him lightly on the shoulder:

'Dad?' He waited a moment, then nudged him harder.

All at once, without even turning to face him properly, his dad began sliding slowly towards him. Then falling.

Malcolm tried pushing him back: his dad was supposed to be ill, not playing games.

'Mum's waiting. We should go for tea. Come on.'

Even trying as hard as he could, he couldn't hold him from slipping further. Not his whole weight.

There was a loud *crack*: his father's head hitting full-force against the edge of the bedside table.

'Dad! Dad!'

Suddenly his mother was standing in the doorway; staring, white-faced. She screamed.

He pushed past her, rushed out of the room and a moment later was back in the kitchen where the Chartbuster Show had started to play the new number five and the table was laid for tea.

He heard her scream again.

The room was exactly the same as before but through the rasping tear in her voice he could feel his father's stubbled cheek still scraping his own, and the boniness of his jaw.

Quickly, before another scream came, he covered his ears. He was standing rigidly still in the centre of the room, facing the silence of the sideboard mirror where there was no screaming, no weight pressing on top of him. Nor the terrible *crack* his father's head had made as he fell. In the mirror everything was ready for them to sit down and eat tea as usual.

He went up to the sideboard and looked closer.

Taking his hands away from his ears, he reached towards the glass where his reflection's hands were already reaching towards his. Their fingertips touched. After a moment's hesitation he pressed harder, breaking through into the silence underneath.

His reflection and himself together, looking out for the first time. As though seeing the room through his reflection's eyes:

Everything in the kitchen happening as it should do. The plates laid out, the chairs in position, the two-bar fire, and you standing by yourself in front of the mirror. You can still hear your mother's screams but as they are on the *outside* now, they can no longer hurt you.

It is time to take your seat at the table and wait for her return.

What had she done wrong?

If she kept holding the Bible she would be safe.

Her slightest movement rubbed her body against her nightdress, against the sheet. Temptation.

Temptation, and then sin. Wickedness.

She'd almost run out of the old woman's room, as if trying to get further and further from the flames of Hell she'd felt touch her.

What had she done wrong?

Over the years she had pared her life down to the most basic elements to keep herself safe. Apart from her Church commitments she never went out in the evening, never had visitors. She'd created a pattern for her life, a routine that protected her. At forty-seven years old she had thought herself beyond danger.

Like always she'd been settled in her armchair by the fire, the door closed, curtains pulled, the reading lamp on. She'd been up since seven and hardly stopped once all day, what with the paperwork, the staff, and over two hours wasted at the Health Board offices. She didn't ask for much. To be left to arrange her evenings in her own way. To close the door, pull the curtains, get settled by the fire, bothering no-one and no-one bothering her.

She'd phoned Margaret in the afternoon to ask if her husband was showing any improvement — did that not count for something? Once she was certain Stella was through in the staffroom watching TV, and the residents in their rooms, she had relaxed. With God's Word for company there should have been nothing to do but keep her eyes open and keep turning the pages. She should have been safe and secure.

She knew the words by heart and had repeated them aloud whenever her attention wandered. That had always worked before. The rest of the room was in half-shadow; all that mattered was the lamplight and her Bible. Had the sound of rain begun she wouldn't even have listened for the patterns it made against the glass; she didn't do that any more. Bed at ten-thirty, and the night hours reduced to a certainty the shape and size of the sleeping-pill she would swallow and be finished with in a moment. That's what should have happened.

From now on she'd take her pills even earlier if need be. Then she could snap her fingers at the rain, the flames could burn her and she would simply turn over and sleep.

Had it been that unexpected phone-call from her sister?

Until then everything had gone just as it should. She'd been reading from the Book of Ruth, whispering a few of the verses aloud every so often to keep herself on course for bed. Her voice was company; it returned her to where she was: sitting beside her own fire, in her own house. That's when the phone rang — if only it had been some relative wanting to visit one of the residents tomorrow, or a new resident, maybe.

She'd answered it in her professional voice:

'Rosehaven Nursing Home. Fiona McBride speaking.'

The instant she realized it was Margaret, and why she was calling, she'd changed to a more personal tone. All in all the conversation had been handled very well. She'd been sympathetic — with her experience she'd known exactly the right questions to ask, and could make the proper responses when required. She'd been patient, too, while her sister told her again and again, over and over, that Peter had been on the mend; that he'd been expected to get up for tea; that the doctor had told her the worst was past; that it was young Malcolm who had found him.

Then came the tears.

Then the same story all over again from the start. She'd been a good listener, though, and by the end had managed to bring Margaret some comfort. Offering to go down for the funeral was one thing, but she shouldn't have suggested they could come up to Edinburgh. It had been a kind thought, of course, but having her sister in the house — having Malcolm, especially — would upset her routine.

And her routine was all she had.

It was only after she'd calmed herself by listening to the even *tick-tick* of the mantelpiece clock that she had she been able to continue reading afterwards. She had never succeeded in making an interesting pattern out of its predictable steady stroke. Unlike rain, for then the wind could always alter its force against the glass to change its sound and sometimes even silence it for several beats at a time. A few more pages and it would have been time to put away her Bible, take her pill and have a last word with Stella before going up to her room.

Then the temptation began:

The upstairs corridors with a table lamp at each landing, and the line of closed doors. Closed doors with their spy-holes for looking in. Closed doors that could open.

She had her routine, and she would stick to it. She'd pressed herself deeper into her chair. Two pills, she decided. Maybe even three, after hearing her sister's sad news.

Pausing outside one of the rooms, turning the handle. The sound of someone breathing.

She'd tried to keep reading, she'd really tried:

'And an angel of the Lord came up—'

Darkness apart from a faint nightlight shining on the bedside table.

'And an angel of the Lord came up from Gilgal—'

Then she began reading aloud:

'And an angel of the Lord came up from Gilgal to Bochim.'

The bedroom would be warm. She would have to move cautiously and make no noise.

'Came up from Gilgal to Bochim and said, I made you to go up out of Israel—'

Being careful not to waken the sleeper.

'Made you go up out of Israel—'

The stillness in the room, the half-darkness, the smell of old age.

'To-go-up-out-of-Israel—'

She'd watched herself put the book aside, switch off the gas fire, and go into the hall. She paused, listened. The only sound was from Stella's TV at the back of the house. She began climbing the stairs.

Then, strangest thing, like she was a little girl again, she'd started climbing the colours. Going from side to side up the stairs, following the pattern on the carpet and being careful not to step in the wrong place. She'd not done that since before Margaret had been born. This evening she'd even gone back twice to retrace her steps, to be quite sure. Forty years ago she'd been terrified to make a mistake. When the sun wasn't shining, or when she'd gone up to her bed alone, the staircase had been a place of terror. No solid ground meant that her foot might sink into nothingness until it disappeared — or, even worse, until she herself disappeared. Every night she'd rushed all the way up, putting as little of her weight as possible on each step, and would be panting when she reached her room, sometimes almost in tears at the relief of having arrived safely. Even sunny days could not be completely trusted. A cloud might pass at any moment, blocking out the light, and the very ground she was standing on might be taken from her.

What had she been doing?

She wasn't a little girl any longer. She was real, the stairs were real and the colours didn't matter any more. Up to the first floor. Breathing quicker already, smiling to herself. Everything was under control. This was an adventure, a harmless walk along an upstairs corridor at night.

Mrs Collins' door?

A quick glance through the spyhole to check the old dear was comfortable. Having a quick glance, that was all she was doing. Nothing more. Quite under control.

But now she'd seen into one of the rooms, seen the ornaments and photographs, the head on the pillow. She should have gone to bed, but she couldn't. She felt more excited, she just *had* to go into one of the rooms and touch the ornaments, examine the photographs.

Where would be the harm?

A glance into the next room and into the next after that, breathing quicker each time. What had she thought she was looking for? She'd stopped and stared at Granny's brass bowl as if she'd never seen it before — standing, as always, at the point where the next flight of stairs began. She just had to put her hand into it. She didn't want to, she just *had* to. She'd asked Mother once how a bowl could hold darkness and in answer Mother had grabbed her hand and forced it into the bowl, saying, 'You want to see how darkness makes things disappear, do you?'

She'd struggled but Mother had been much stronger. For a moment this evening she'd thought her hand might really disappear. Then she'd dashed up to the second floor: every step taken so carefully and silently along the corridor.

Mrs Southwick's door; Mr Blackwood's; Mrs Tait's.

At the top stair of the third-floor landing she'd almost slipped. She rested there for a moment, held the banisters to steady herself. That was to be her last chance for safety: to take her pill, two pills, three, however many she had to, make her way to her room and to sleep. But then she would have had to let go the banisters, unclasp her fingers, turn and force herself back down every step she'd already come up. She should have known what was right, and what was temptation. Standing at the top of the stairs, hesitating whether or not to go further along the corridor and into one of the rooms: that hesitation should have been enough to have told her. That sense of longing, of expectation and excitement — of desire.

The hall clock chimed the hour. She had clung to the sound of each separate chime to keep herself where she was, and not go forward. Eight—nine—ten—

Then, silence.

Only the polished wood to grasp onto, curving upwards under her palm, arching her fingers, pushing her forwards almost, towards the darkened corridor, towards the closed doors. This floor was the worst: the bedridden, the sick-and-simple. Her hands were trembling, sweat was trickling down her back. There were six doors: three on either side.

Mrs Davidson; Mrs Connaught; Mrs Byrd.

Mr Wells; Mrs Goldfire. The very last room was unoccupied.

Rather than go in there with its bed stripped, its dressing-table cleared of ornaments, she would have started her search all over again. Was that where all temptation led? To be trapped for ever in one moment of the night, rushing from floor to floor, room to room?

She took a deep breath, then tried each door in turn. Pausing long enough until she was certain: Mrs Davidson's? Mrs Connaught's? Mrs Byrd's? Leaning against the door frames to rest, but she had to keep going. Outside Mrs Goldfire's. Yes, the same panelled wood, the same paintwork. And yet, feeling so different from the others. As if she recognized it. She had to go in. The certainty of its being the right room had been such relief that she was almost shaking as she began turning the handle.

Having closed the door soundlessly behind her, she had stood for a moment perfectly still, then switched on the bed light. Mrs Goldfire was lying on her back with her bedcap half on the pillow, half on her nearly bald scalp, while she breathed lightly but steadily; her right hand was out of the covers.

For that last second it had seemed as if she were watching herself standing in the old woman's room. As if all her life until then she had been merely the observer of another's longing. And suddenly there was no *other*. Had she, in dreams perhaps, rehearsed to perfection what she was about to do?

She moved with a sureness that thrilled her. Firstly, the photographs. A wedding in black and white, a group of children, a bungalow with a couple and a dog outside. She glanced at them one by one, running her fingers over the glass and the metal frames; tracing out someone's features, a prominent forehead, a smile.

Then she laid them face down.

From behind her came the sound of the old woman's thin strengthless breathing. In the dressing-table mirror the bed light showed one side of Mrs Goldfire's face lined and mottled, the other in shadow. Next came the ornaments: a small china cat; a dark wooden box containing a few earrings, a cheap-looking bracelet and a necklace; a fan spread open to reveal a Spanish dancer with 'A Present from Seville' printed on the plastic handle. She picked it up, snapped it shut, opened it and fanned herself while she took a few steps up and down the space between the bed and the chest of drawers.

The charm bracelet had a broken clasp. She weighted the heavy necklace in her hand but felt, even then, it was the wrong colour. Luckily there were a few scent bottles. She unscrewed each top in turn and had a smell — old women's perfumes. The eau-de-Cologne made her almost dizzy with excitement. She breathed it in, closed her eyes briefly, and *there*, without any effort on her part, was her mother's bedroom once more; with its curtains open to show that bright September morning ten years ago.

Another deep breath and she could make out the figure lying with its head on the pillow, its hand stretched out towards her. She sighed, smiled to herself, then replaced the stopper and put the small glass bottle in precisely the same spot it had been before. Two steps, three, and she was holding the covers, the stitched hem of the sheet. She must get onto her knees. She must press her face into the smell of the blankets, no longer disgusting as it had been all those years ago, but sweet. Intoxicating. She fumbled for the old lady's hand. She knew exactly what she had to say:

'I'm sorry I didn't come sooner. Really sorry.' Whispering while she caressed the old woman's open palm. 'I wanted to, you must understand. More than anything I wanted to come to you. But I wasn't sure.' She squeezed each finger in turn, very gently.

The old lady's hand was resting lightly on her head. Yes, that was what she had come for. That was how it should have been all those years ago. The smell of the bedclothes, the frailty of the hand, the slow breathing, and the closeness between them — that, most of all. The bony fingers lay unsteadily on her hair, then began caressing her face. Nothing else mattered, only the touch of that hand on her cheek, smoothing the hair away from her eyes, tracing out the shape of her mouth. Nothing else mattered except the tenderness. The love.

There was a moment of such utter peace she had almost wept with gratitude to be there; surely that was true forgiveness. Then the moment passed.

She felt her mouth going dry; her tongue was sliding against her teeth. She swallowed, then gripped the old woman's hand tighter. That was when her nipples began hardening, her thighs aching to be touched. She turned and almost ran from the room, her whole body burning, burning.

Wickedness, wickedness, wickedness.

Lying back in her own bed now she could see the ceiling curved above her by her tears.

3

From now on, if you manage to keep everything *outside*, there'll be no pain.

Your mother's in tears during most of the funeral and your Aunt Fiona goes on and on in her 'holy' voice about whether you're all right or not. And you are — so long as they and everything else stay *outside*.

Afterwards you're taken to the Townhead Hotel for the first time in your life. The front hall's bigger than your sitting-room, with a blue carpet crisscrossed by the dark paths made by people's wet shoes. If it was your house they'd all get a row. The coats, scarves and umbrellas stacked in a huge old-fashioned stand have begun steaming in the warmth. Then it's down a long corridor past swing doors marked 'Private' and into a room set aside for your aunts, uncles, cousins and the friends of your father. Here the blue carpet seems even thicker, hushing the room and making the people as they come in speak quietly or say nothing at all.

Because you are the youngest you are passed among the adults, and asked what you are up to these days, what height you are, what school's like, and told that now you are the man of the house you will have to look after your mother. You never get the chance to ask anything back. Some of them want to know how you are feeling. When you tell them you're fine, they look very seriously at you, saying you cannot be expected to understand, poor boy. Telling them you're sad is even worse: they start patting you. What is the right answer? To your mother most of them say how sorry they are, what a tragedy it is and that she must be very tired.

Tired, maybe you should try saying that? Grownups are always saying they're tired, even in the mornings; when you are tired you fall asleep. You should try it, though, and see what happens.

Immediately the tea and sandwiches are served, everyone begins talking more loudly and the questions come to a stop. You're left to get on with your Coke and as many sandwiches as you can claim without being noticed. You eat, drink and finish. The large window next to you is a solid wall of condensation so you can hardly see out. The noise seems to be getting even louder. You press your hand to the glass to make the mist vanish. Now you can see what's happening in the street. It's like watching TV with cartoon characters being jerked across the gap you've made for them. There's a house painter in his overalls and no coat getting soaked through; a man so bicycle-caped you can't make out his face, only that it's all beard; a woman who's all shopping-bags and a brolly she can't hold straight. You're always getting told not to sit too near the telly, but it doesn't matter here. The characters rush on and off the screen so fast it makes you laugh. You should show your mum; it might cheer her up a little.

Suddenly you catch sight of a flock of birds passing very high above. They don't seem to be moving at all, really — as if they'd been painted on to a piece of sky that's being pulled along in slow motion. You wipe the glass to make the gap bigger. The birds are keeping a perfect V-shaped formation. You leave your seat to follow them along the edge of the window, rubbing the glass clear, pushing your way past chairs and other people's tables. When you reach the far wall you stand and watch them disappear. There's nothing you can do but stare at the empty piece of sky they've left behind.

'What are you looking at?' Your uncle from Paisley is standing beside you, smoking a cigarette.

'Nothing.' It's true, the birds have gone and there is nothing any more.

He doesn't speak for a moment, then starts on the same list of questions as everybody else: what you are up to, your height, the school, the man of the house. When he asks how you are feeling you're ready to tell him:

'Tired.'

There is a long pause, a silent nod then, in a different tone of voice than anyone has ever used to you before, he says that he understands. The right answer at last, but you're careful not to smile.

The meal finished, Aunt Fiona, who's been organizing you, your mother and everyone else since she arrived, drives you home.

The two of them sit in the front and your aunt talks about the good turn-out; that the service went well; that they were lucky with the weather. Your mother says 'yes' every so often. Now that everything's happening *outside*, it's easy just to turn the sound down and stop listening.

The rain will make it harder for any snow to lie. Last year about this time you went sledging every day for a week.

'Aunt Fiona is asking you a question, Malcolm.'

Before she looks round you close your eyes and pretend to be asleep. A half-snore to make it more convincing. If she speaks to you again, you will have to pretend to wake. You turn the sound up:

'Malcolm, Aunt Fiona's—'

'It's all right, Margaret. Let him sleep. He's had a very difficult day. Remember how tired we were after Mother's funeral?'

Your mother hasn't answered. Still keeping your eyes closed you will have to turn the sound up further in case you miss something. A moment later your aunt speaks again:

'We were both exhausted that day, weren't we?'

Aunt Fiona sounds like a teacher trying to help a pupil to the right answer, but still your mother doesn't reply. After another pause your aunt begins:

'Margaret, surely you remember how—?'

'I remember our mother's funeral very clearly, thank you, Fiona.' Your mother is angry. You turn the volume up full to catch everything. 'Evidently much better than you.'

For a moment it looks as if there is going to be a row but, instead, there is silence until you reach your home.

Once in the door Aunt Fiona makes a cup of tea, and the three of you sit at the kitchen table with the curtains pulled, even though it's not really dark. Your mother's stopped crying but whenever you catch her eye she seems to start all over again. You're not meaning to make her cry; you don't want her to. Instead you glance away, only to catch sight of her in the mirror, side on. She looks different there: still your mother, but as if she was living her life without you.

'And do you think you will like Edinburgh?' Aunt Fiona has reached over and laid her hand firmly on your shoulder. To secure her black gauzy scarf loosely at her neck she is wearing something that looks like a swollen paper-clip, but made from the same shiny metal as her stapled-on earrings.

When you don't reply immediately she digs her fingers into your shoulder:

'Do you think you will like coming to stay with me in Edinburgh?'

You can see your mum trying to give you an encouraging smile. You smile back and say you are looking forward to it. A phrase you've often heard people use. Another first-time try. It works. Aunt Fiona nods and releases you.

There'll be no chance of hearing any of 'The Best from the US' tonight. Especially not with Aunt Fiona there. The next hour passes very slowly. You're expected to sit, be seen and be silent. Any time you've reached for a comic or for something else to do, your mum's said: 'Not today, please, Malcolm,' and Aunt Fiona's looked at you very, very hard. Finally you're sent to bed, early.

'A goodnight kiss for your favourite aunt?' Turning towards you but without reaching any closer, Aunt Fiona is really asking you to stand up, go round to where she's sitting and put your lips on the side of her powdered cheek. The first time that happened, when you were much younger, you'd kissed her on the mouth just as you usually did your mum; and she'd jerked back immediately, her face very red and angry. If you kissed her like that today she couldn't be angry with you, not just after your dad's funeral. Her mouth is lipstick-red, but you'll only need to touch it for a second. She'll be so angry at not being allowed to be angry, she might go even redder than last time.

You mustn't smile at her as you approach. If you catch her eye she might guess what's coming and turn away. So, instead, you should look as if you're concentrating on that part of her cheek where she's expecting the goodnight kiss.

Almost there. She's leaning a little towards you. Her perfume's not light and flowery like your mum's, but heavy, like a closed room. She nods slightly:

'Goodnight, Malcolm.'

As planned, you look to the side to mislead her, then quickly glance back, take aim, lock onto target. Fire.

Direct hit. What a look in her eyes: a direct hit, right enough!

'Goodnight, Aunt Fiona.' You turn away, pretending nothing unusual's happened; she's jerked back and gone red again exactly like the first time. She's wanting to say something, she's raging, but having to choke herself back. You mustn't burst out laughing, or even smile.

As you leave the room you glance back to see what she's doing. Your mum's talking to her but she's not really listening. She's glaring hard at the place where you'd been standing, as if in another dimension a different Aunt Fiona from the one who's not allowed to get angry with you today was shouting at a different you from the one who's just come from his dad's funeral. She's angry-angry-red, all right.

Mission accomplished, now back to base.

You go to your room and a few minutes later your mother comes through to say goodnight. She sits on the edge of your bed and talks first about your dad and how you'll both miss him. She smooths your hair back and asks how you are feeling.

'All right,' you say, 'but tired.'

The right answer.

Then she tells you your dad didn't really suffer any pain and that in a way he's still with you. Her voice is very sad — is she about to start crying again? Close to, as she draws away from you and stands up, you can see the beginnings of tears, but they won't upset you. You don't feel bad even when you remember going into his room and finding him. It's not happening now. It's on the *outside*, like the sadness in her voice.

Finally she bends down to kiss you goodnight, then leaves. The door shuts behind her, *click*. Next comes the kitchen door closing. Then, nothing. Usually when your mother went back through to the kitchen there was the sound of her and your dad talking, or laughter from the TV. Or some music, maybe. But not now. Dead silence now, like when the minister had switched off the music tape to start the funeral this afternoon. One minute there had been loud organ music surrounding you, its rhythm exactly in time to your breathing, and the next there was nothing. You had to force yourself to start breathing afterwards.

With the light off, your room is like an old black-and-white movie, the brightness turned so far down that you can only just make out the shape of the wardrobe, the tea chest holding your toys, the mirror which seems to flicker here and there with lighter dots; the Virgin Radio poster. The window frame, too, seems blurred and flickering at the edges with faint light from outside, while the glass itself is total darkness. For a moment it's as if by sitting up and staring straight over at the window you are really looking down onto a pool of water, a pool of very dirty water covered with ice. Or you're in a submarine — deep, deep down in the ocean where there's no light. That's what it feels like suddenly: you're fathoms deep in the darkness, with the water pushing against the sides. You can almost hear the metal hull creak with the pressure, and at any moment a monster fish, all teeth, scales and blinded eyes, might hurl itself in a fury against the porthole, shattering it.

You're going deeper and so the pressure's building up, forcing the dark water between the glass and its frame. It's started leaking into the room. If you went over to the window and held your hands there, the water would seep between your fingers. It's covering the carpet now, covering your soldiers, racing cars, your moon base. The dirty water is rising around your bed, getting deeper and deeper. You are going to drown. You have to hold your breath. Your legs are going numb. Now your arms, your fists. Your chest is bursting.

You want to scream out loud—

4

Fiona sat at her sister's kitchen table, resting. This was the first moment she'd had time to herself, to think. At least she was getting away from the temptation of another night visit. She could picture herself kneeling there in that old woman's room — and hated what she was seeing.

Ever since she arrived yesterday she'd been looking after Margaret, looking after Malcolm, making sure everything went smoothly. Most tiring of all, she'd been polite to her sister's friends and relations, complete strangers to her. A nice enough service; her sister had wept all the way through and was in no state to thank the minister properly afterwards. Fortunately Fiona had noticed and been able to see to that herself, so there was no harm done. Malcolm was too young to understand what was happening. And yet, though she'd been ready with a pocketful of clean hankies, he'd been a brave little soldier. Not one tear. It would have been a kindness to have put her arm around him at some points during the service — she was his favourite aunt, after all — but he had borne up well.

Considering this was a rented cottage, Margaret was lucky to find herself with such a good oak table: a tight-grained wood, not like sprawling pine, but true and straight. She couldn't have continued being nice to people a moment longer. Her hands took the weight of her head, the table the weight of elbows. Her eyes were closed and she didn't have to open them. Much more tired than after Mother's funeral, where she'd seen to all the arrangements by herself to keep things simple, and save her pregnant little sister from upset. No effort to remain dry-eyed at that sending off: the effort had been to keep from shouting out 'Amen' or even cheering as Mother's coffin slid from sight. While the minister had been droning on she'd run her fingers along the patterns made on the shiny wooden pew. The grain lay under a hard-set varnish. At the bevelled rim a small transparent drop had gathered, suspended frozen over the edge. She'd picked at it and had almost managed to get down to the wood by the time everyone stood for the hymn. With a last effort she'd tried to snap it off but it was too hard. That was when she'd noticed her little sister was actually crying.

Margaret was taking her time putting Malcolm to bed. He'd been so tired when kissing her goodnight he'd accidentally kissed her on the mouth instead. Just as well she wasn't the kind of woman who encouraged that sort of thing. Should she have given him a hug? But boys got very embarrassed sometimes.

She flattened both her palms on the table and followed the straight-running grain as far forward as she could. With her face pressed down on the surface her fingertips reached to the other side, just and no more. The wood felt smooth. Her fingers touching the opposite edge, her arms at full stretch: she could rest. There was no temptation here.

Immediately she'd returned home from Mother's funeral, before even taking off her coat, she'd gone upstairs to the empty bedroom. It had been raining. She went over to close the window left open for airing. Having binned everything the day before, she stepped wide to avoid the stripped mattress, the bedside cabinet cleared of junk. The lace curtain kept flapping in the draught and the window-sill was spattered with wet. That's how it was: icy-cold and clean. Mother had been completely scoured out of the room. The window pulled down and snibbed, she'd stared out at the rain. Without wanting to she'd thought about that moment many times since. Had she really been about to cry then? She'd been unsure about turning around. Not that she really expected to see Mother's ghost stretched out on the mattress, or reflected in the tilted mirror on the dressing table. But she had been afraid. Those few threatened tears had made her afraid.

'I hate you, I hate you — you evil bitch!' That's what Margaret had shouted at Mother before finally leaving home. Mother had just laughed. 'You're evil! Evil!' her sister had screamed over the top banisters. Mother came down the last few steps into the hall, smiling: 'Ah, Fiona. Cat got your tongue, has it? It's a dangerous cat that one, and lives in the dark.' She'd stopped, rapped her knuckles on her head, then pointed up towards Margaret: 'I like to hear my girls speak out like that. I want them to feel they can tell me anything, confide in me.' She had wanted to scream at Mother as well, but she had said nothing. Mother had leant close and whispered: 'A cat's claws must scratch one day, and if they don't scratch me, that only leaves you. So watch out.' Then she'd taken Fiona's hand and ran her fingernails down her cheek: 'Not a mark, you're the lucky one, eh!'

During the final months Mother had become weak and tearful. It was a real joy to ignore her pathetic whining and clinging, and instead, in what was to become her best professional manner, she'd ask if she was comfortable. Did she need a warmer bedjacket, perhaps, or would she like to be read to? Sometimes, having seen the look of helplessness on Mother's face, she'd come out of the sick-room and feel like doing cartwheels down the corridor.

She pressed her face harder against the table. If she let her arms open fanwise, would they touch the corners? She tried — a bit like doing the breast stroke across very hard water — and slowly they began arcing down to her sides. Straining, she inched her fingers a little more. How much further could she go? The table was solid, with four legs set on the floor, and the floor of the cottage set on the very surface of the earth. If she pressed all her weight down, surely the earth couldn't give way?

5

The dressing-table, the wardrobe, your soldiers, racing cars, the moon base, your football boots, skates, comics — everything looks ordinary and the same. But you know it's not, you know that from now on you will have to make things *outside* happen exactly as they should.

In a few minutes you will go through to have breakfast, then you will put on your scarf. You'll take your jacket from the hook at the back of the door; you'll shout goodbye to your mum and Aunt Fiona, telling them to look after each other until you get back. You'll cut across the garden, climb through the gap in the fence and go to play with Sonny. At twelve you'll come home for dinner. If everything happens as it should, you will be safe.

It's been snowing already and there might be more to come. There are clouds beyond Stuart's Hill. Dirty yellow clouds, which is a good sign. Everywhere's white. Even the fence-posts and the wire are frosted over. Your gang-hut, the old summerhouse in Sonny's garden, should really be called a winterhouse now. With its circular walls and its pointed roof all snow, it looks like an enormous ice-cream cone set upside down. So long as it doesn't melt when you're inside. Not that there's much chance; it's freezing. That's the good news. The bad news you can see immediately you turn into Sonny's yard: Gregor's there. He should be down at Robson's farm playing computer games on the big screen. Instead, he'll be telling you what to do all morning.

Sonny's looking straight at you:

'Sorry about your dad.'

You nod. Your footprints have made a ragged-looking trail in the frost from your front door to where you are now.

'But it's all right you coming out now?' he adds.

Gregor's paying you no attention, he's kicking the ground to see how hard it is.

'Yes. My aunt's staying just now. From Edinburgh. She's helping my mum.'

Sonny gives you a quick smile:

'That one? You said she was a bit—'

'She is,' you smile back. You both laugh. 'Anyway, it means I can come out — seeing she's here.'

'That's something.' Then, after a short pause, Sonny continues:

'You can borrow my Gameboy if you want.'

You are just about to suggest he gets it when Gregor butts in to say he's sorry about your dad and that he expects it can't be easy. Then he gives the ground another kick:

'Right, this is what we're doing.'

A few minutes later the garden's been split between the three of you, Gregor getting most. The clouds and any aeroplane passing will belong to each of you in turn. You're the youngest but today you get more because your dad's dead. Part of the lawn, some flower pots, two rows of raspberry canes and the sky that's directly above. Gregor'll attack you first, so you should put the flowerpots in order, and get the gravel ready.

'Start attacking on the count of ten,' he shouts. 'Ten, nine, eight, seven…'

Suddenly it's begun to snow. A few heavy flakes but there'll be more to come. Lots more. A blizzard, maybe. Half a blizzard already. The counting stops.

'Into the hut, or they'll call us in.'

While the other two go through the half-empty paint tins, rakes, trowels and brushes — these need checking over since last time — you stare out at the snow. All at once it's as if you're both outside and inside the summerhouse at the same time: in the complete silence surrounding you as falling snow. And in the noise the two brothers make: scraping tools and metal cans over the floor. Silence and noise: which are you part of?

Which are you making happen?

Gregor's started talking about last night's *Space Precinct*. The hero's ship was trapped in a sector of empty space with aliens on all sides. You don't like Gregor so you turn the sound down and stop listening.

The other parts of the garden can be used as the desert, the jungle, or whatever, but the gang-hut never stands for anything else. Robson's farm and the low road are pressed flat against the window like a newly-done painting. If you touch the glass you will smudge them. That is the *outside* and must be kept there exactly as it is. Shut your eyes, or everything just beyond what you can see will close in upon the hut, crushing you.

Gregor's given you a sudden push:

'You falling asleep?'

'No, I was just pretending.' The summerhouse is safe. It must be. Nothing can touch you here.

The only way to keep the *outside* as it should be is to tell things as they should be. Even the drowning last night: if you tell it differently, it will be different.

'I can fly,' you say.

Gregor keeps talking.

'Last night I held my breath, then flew from my bed right up to the ceiling.'

Sonny is looking at you and wants to hear more, but not Gregor. Why doesn't he go to Robson's? Much better for everyone.

You go and stand in the centre of the summerhouse:

'Right to the ceiling.'

At last Gregor turns to you:

'Well, and what's up with you?'

You shouldn't reply immediately but wait till you've got their full attention. Several seconds pass.

'Well then?'

'I'm telling you. I flew all the way up to the ceiling.'

'Dreamer. Sleep–flying, was it?'

'But I did, I did.'

Gregor taps the side of his head. Just because your dad's dead, he thinks you're mad.

'I did. Right up to the ceiling. Then all round my bedroom.'

'How long did it take?' At least Sonny believes you.

'I don't know.'

'What do you mean, you don't know?' Gregor looks at you very hard. 'If you flew, you must know how long it took.'

'I don't. It just happened, then stopped happening. I didn't look at a clock. I was flying round and round.'

'You said you went straight up before.'

'Yes I did. But you see—'

Sonny is looking encouragingly:

'Yes. Did anyone *see* you, maybe?'

'I don't know. They might have done, if they'd been looking in.'

Gregor gets to his feet. 'For someone who says he's been flying round and round his own bedroom, you don't seem to know much about it.' He goes over to the window and starts rubbing away at the condensation.

Sonny's still interested:

'What was it like, flying?'

Now you can tell them how it really should have been:

'Like drowning, but only at first. Then it was like floating.' You're answering Sonny, but you know Gregor will be listening. 'No, better than that. It was like diving, then swimming underwater for ages and ages. Only you didn't need any water.'

Gregor turns round abruptly:

'If there wasn't any water, you couldn't swim.'

'Yes, but if you could.'

'I don't believe you. Anyway, the snow's stopped.' He opens the door and goes into the garden. Clever-clogs. He's started to walk off in the direction of the raspberry canes.

'Just you watch,' you call out. You know what you have to do: quickly wipe the snow from a couple of boxes, put them against the summerhouse wall and start climbing. The wood is damp and rotting in places, but you'll manage. Sonny gives you a shove up as you reach for the rone-pipe. It holds. Gregor's watching now. Pull yourself onto the slates, and the rest will be easy.

Your hands are covered with green slime from the wood; it's getting difficult to grip. Holding on tight, you feel around with your foot for the ledge on top of the window. If it takes your weight you'll be able to stand just as steadily as on the roof. All you'll need will be one last push.

You've done it. The ledge, and you're in position. You should stop for a moment to look around, to prepare yourself. How high you are: white roofs and white countryside as far as you can see, smoke from the chimneys rising straight into the still air.

'You all right?' Sonny calls up to you.

'Fine. Getting myself ready.'

The two brothers are staring up at you. Take a deep breath, just as you did last night. You held it for as long as you could — then let go, and rose up towards the ceiling. That's how you're telling it now, and so that's how the *outside* must happen.

The roof is very steep. Wet and slippery where you've rubbed away the snow. You should pretend you're in your bedroom; maybe even shut your eyes.

You are getting lighter. It's going to work. You must keep your eyes shut to let the silence come as close as you can. And then, when you're ready, let go.

You must stand to your full height. Spread your arms out wide. Gregor and Sonny are both watching you. You are about to fly.

6

It was ten-thirty. Another few hours and she would have to leave for Edinburgh. Already she could picture the upstairs corridors, the closed doors…

She had to get herself back into her routine: when she returned, there would be her evening meal, reading or the TV, then her sleeping-pill and straight to bed. If she started now to plan things, and stuck exactly to what she'd planned, there would be no possibility of temptation. She should make a list and keep to it, item by item.

This is what she would do:

- On with her coat and warm boots.
- Out of the cottage and left along the low road.
- Turn right, and up to the Post Office shop. (If she met anyone on the way she would say a polite 'Good morning' and pass on.)
- Push open the Post Office door.
- 'Good morning' to whoever was there. (If there were other customers and she had to wait, she would glance at the postcard/newspaper rack. She'd be quite all right.)
- Up to the counter. The shopkeeper was called Mrs Doyle. Or was it Mrs Douglas? Mrs Doyle. Another 'Good morning', then a polite: 'Do you have any spare cardboard boxes, please?' *Empty* cardboard boxes would be better. 'Do you have any empty cardboard boxes, please?' (No small talk, no explanations. Mrs Doyle would understand why they were needed.)

- Get the boxes and leave. Less than a minute in and out.
- Return here to Margaret's to finish packing away Peter's effects.
- A light lunch, and drive back to Edinburgh in time to catch up with the last two days' work.
- A restful evening by the fire. Some Bible, some TV.
- Her sleeping-pill.
- Straight to bed.

And that would be that.

She stood up and called through to the next room:

'Margaret, the snow's almost stopped, so I'm off to get some boxes. Back shortly.'

On with the coat and warm boots.

The sudden cold immediately she stepped outside. The snow crunching underfoot like powdered glass. The harsh brightness scratched at her skin; a gust of wind and it would have been cutting into her face. Like going into Mother's room again, into its icy cleanness. That empty room, with the rain falling outside.

This was Margaret's village. Here was the path to the main road, to the Post Office shop. She was going to get some boxes for packing Peter's effects. With her day already planned she should relax and enjoy the walk. It had been snowing heavily. Stuart's Hill, with the big house where somebody lived, was completely white. A deep breath of cold, cold air. There was no empty bedroom any more, no weather outside clawing to get to her. She smiled to herself and began walking.

She'd hardly gone halfway when she just had to stop and admire the view. A pretty-as-a-picture village scene in winter. Snow-covered lane, the dykes smoothed white with the slightest *chiaroscuro* effect where the wind had exposed some stonework, the trees quickly sketched in. And the farm. Robson's farm, it was called. A working concern, to judge by the tractor-marks in and out of the yard. A fall of snow in Edinburgh, and the streets quickly became no more than gullies of dirty slush. So she was lucky to have the chance of so pleasant a short stroll here. She'd pass the village cross and soon be at the shop.

Walking quickly:

Left-right, left-right. Quick-march, keep-warm. Left-right, left-right.

She'd been counting before she stopped:

Ninety-four, ninety-five, ninety-six, ninety-seven...

Keep going. The shop, at last. Pushing the door open. No-one else there. The bell dinged.

The shopkeeper — it wasn't Mrs Doyle, but she'd still continue as planned — wore a yellow nylon apron over her blouse and jersey. The woman, whoever she was, had looked up from sorting through a pile of newspapers:

'Good morning. Cold out, eh?'

No small talk, no explanations. 'Good morning,' and she asked politely for some empty boxes. The woman went to get them. Everything was under control.

Mrs Whoever-it-was returned with four large cartons:

'Pass my condolences on to Mrs Watson. I'll not trouble her in her sorrow, but she knows she's welcome to drop by when she feels up to it. Are you stopping long yourself?'

'Unfortunately I have to get back to Edinburgh by—'

The bell dinged. Someone had just come in.

The postman.

He had started speaking to her:

'Manage all right? I can give you a hand if you want.'

The boxes were awkward to hold — one was already slipping. The shopkeeper was looking at her. The postman was looking at her. Should she finish her reply to the woman, or answer the postman — or just smile and go?

Turning back to the shopkeeper:

'By late afternoon.' Then to the postman:

'I'll manage fine, thank you.' She took a firmer grip of the boxes and moved towards the door.

'Are you sure?'

'It's kind of you to offer.' A smile for the postman. A smile for the shopkeeper. The same goodbye to be shared between them.

The postman was holding the door for her and looking concerned:

'I was sorry to hear about your brother-in-law. A young man, too.'

Why couldn't they let her go? She was busy, very busy. 'Yes.'

But they were waiting for her to say something more.

'The doctor himself said Mr Watson had been getting better.'

They were both still staring at her. More?

'My sister was expecting him to get up for tea. Hoping, I mean,' she added, 'that he'd get up. But he wasn't able to.'

That hadn't sounded quite right, but maybe it was enough. Another goodbye, and then out.

The sun was reflected on the snow with a sharpness that hurt her eyes. At the farm she turned down the low road where the whiteness had not yet been trampled into slush and the only footprints were the ones she herself had made when coming to the shop. Through a small courtyard with an ornamental pump; centre-piece for someone's flowerbed. The cottages on either side had their front-room lights on. Not much privacy.

Her footprints were coming to meet her. She began stepping into them: right foot into the left print, and heel to toe. The boxes kept slipping; she needed a firmer grip, her fingers were going numb with the cold. Less than fifty steps more:

Left-right, left-right, quick-march, keep-warm, left-right, left-right.

In her house there were twenty-eight steps from the downstairs hall to the bedroom that had been hers for twelve years — until Margaret came along.

Now it was thirty-seven to her own room.

She tucked one of the boxes more firmly under her arm and kept walking. Was she cancelling the footprints out by reversing her steps so exactly? She almost glanced back over her shoulder to check that the snow really had remained marked, but stopped herself in time — what a silly idea. More to the point, the boxes were getting ever harder to carry. Just beyond the two cottages she had to stop to take a better grip. There was no wind and the snow seemed to have drawn all sound into itself. The burn running beside the path had been frozen into gradual silence. A winter landscape of snow, stone, slate and bare trees: like an old black-and-white photograph. She could easily imagine a little girl somewhere quietly looking through the old photograph album she's found. One of the pictures that has caught her eye could be this very scene here: this stretch of unfamiliar countryside covered in snow. She herself could be there too, pointing out things in the photograph. Together the two of them examine every detail. They can count four, five, six crows like burn marks on the white of the next field. The hedgerow is stripped to thorn and twig; here and there an abandoned nest can be made out. All at once they stop what they're doing, hold their breath and listen: there is the sound of footsteps approaching out in the corridor. She snatches the album from the girl and snaps it shut. She has to hide it quickly. Quickly.

The cold wind had gusted suddenly, making her shiver. What nonsense. She shivered again; she was wasting time standing here.

One of the crows lifted itself awkwardly into the air, flapping its wings until it steadied and began to soar above the field, then turned in line to the neighbour's garden—

And there was Malcolm: standing perfectly motionless on the roof of an old shed, his arms outstretched. He no longer looked like a small boy, but strong and powerful. She stopped herself crying out. An unexpected noise would distract him and make him lose his balance. But what did he think he was doing? She took a step in his direction and watched him rise into the air for a split-second before tumbling to the ground.

'Malcolm!'

He didn't seem to hear. As small boys do, he bounced to his feet almost at once and wandered off with his friends.

Supposing he'd been *her* child? Supposing he'd landed on concrete? Broken his leg? Split his head open? She'd have looked after him. She'd have nursed him and cared for him. Margaret might have burst into tears, but *she*'d have known what to do.

Enough time wasted. She walked quickly towards the house. The front gate was stuck shut. She kicked at the wooden frame, kicked it again, then, without letting go the boxes, wrenched it up and down until the catch gave. She hurried in the front door.

Clearing out a deceased's effects was something she'd done a score of times. All part of the job: illness created work. A sad event merely came down to putting things into plastic bags and cardboard boxes. If Margaret had some bin bags handy they could be finished in half an hour.

The bedroom first: the chest of drawers, the wardrobe, laundry. Clothes were always the easiest.

Then the hall cupboard, for coats and shoes. His work boots at the back door, his cap and jacket on the hook, his wellingtons.

The bathroom: his shaving stuff, hairbrush, comb, toothbrush, medicines.

'You'll need to keep his insurance papers, social security, health card and the like. We'll put them on the dressing table for the present, but you must go through them.' An encouraging smile: clearing out wasn't so hard once you got started.

A portable TV was still facing the end of his bed; through to the living-room with it. Everything else stuffed into the last bag, ready to be put out.

'I wish I still smoked.' Margaret had sat down on the mattress. 'This would be the perfect moment to light up. Maybe I could just sit, breathe and pretend.'

No. A deceased's effects would not pack themselves away, and the job had to be finished before Malcolm appeared.

'Now, do you want to keep any of this?' A drawerful of old photographs and letters.

So many small things lying around. His cigarettes on the chest of drawers; his lighter. A tiny model yacht on the bedside table.

'Is this Malcolm's?'

Her sister started to cry. Peter had been holding the toy yacht in his hand when they found him — was that what she was saying?

Did she want it, or not? They had to keep to schedule or else they would upset Malcolm when he came in. Was there a neighbour who could use the tool-kit? And what about his fishing gear?

The slam of the kitchen door. Malcolm was back, but they were finished — perfect timing.

'Mum?'

'We're in here, Malcolm.'

He'd brought in the cold with him. 'Hello. It's freezing out there, Mum.'

Margaret was too upset to be expected to discuss the weather. So Fiona would do her best to help:

'Malcolm, we were looking at the small boat here.' She held it out to show him. 'Did you give it to your dad?'

He shrugged:

'He must have found it, or something. Mum, are we eating soon?'

Margaret stood up. 'I'd better get things started. Go and wash your hands.'

Malcolm rushed off.

'Thanks for being such a help, Fiona. I really wasn't ready to do all that by myself.' She left.

A help? When she'd done almost everything? But Fiona would not make a fuss. Her sister just wasn't herself at the moment.

She was still holding the yacht: red sails, a green hull, an inch long at most, the paint a bit thin and flaking off. When her hand closed around it, there was a sharp stab of pain — the mast. Her brother-in-law had been holding it when he died. Was that the last thing he had been aware of, its sharpness cutting into him like this?

She squeezed her fist hard on the metal as hard as she could bear; and then even harder.

7

You have to go out — now Aunt Fiona's driven off to Edinburgh, that's what happens next. You're supposed to rush out and play in the snow until you're so tired when you come home you'll go to bed and fall asleep immediately, and be safe. But your mother won't let you — she's changing what's supposed to come next. She's sitting in front of the fire not even doing anything, and wanting you to sit as well.

'No, Malcolm. I said no and I mean no. Maybe Sonny would like to come here instead.'

You have to stop her.

'Dad would have let me go.'

She flinches as if you'd slapped her across the face. You glare at her.

'Malcolm, you don't know what you're saying.' She's almost in tears. You've made her cry only once before, when you fell from a tree in Sonny's garden and hurt yourself. But this is different. Just words.

'Come here, Malcolm.' Her voice sounds wobbly.

You shouldn't move, you shouldn't speak. Words, and now silence. Is she crying yet? If you move slightly to one side you'll be able to see her face more clearly.

'Please, Malcolm. Come here.' She's stretched her hand towards you. 'Please.'

You keep watching her. If you stay exactly as you are, you might make her cry.

'Malcolm.' The pleading in her voice is trying to pull you nearer.

Every muscle rigid, and with your teeth clenched to stop yourself speaking: she's *outside*, she can't hurt you. Let her cry.

She's opened her arms to hold you. Having got to her feet, she's taken a step towards you.

Your arms and legs must be made hard, mirror-hard. Your face, mirror-hard. You cannot risk the touch of her hand or the gentleness in her voice, or else everything will rush into you again; everything as it was just before you entered the mirror's silence. You have to keep her out.

You're hardly able to breathe. Face, chest, hands, arms, legs — rigid. If you move, you might smash into pieces.

'Dad — would — have—'

'Please, Malcolm.'

Louder, to be heard above the mirror-silence:

'Dad — would — have — let—'

She's coming towards you.

You can't let her any nearer. All your strength, you must shout:

'*Dad* would have let me go.'

Then you run from the room.

Sonny's come over without his Gameboy because Gregor's playing with it. Instead he's brought a small bottle and two old-fashioned pens.

'My dad gave it to me just now and said it's good fun. Better than pressing buttons, he said.'

Better or not, a pen nib's a lot more work than a computer. You have to keep dipping it into the invisible ink and, even then, every letter can be scratched only a bit at a time.

And the paper keeps getting torn.

There's a prod in your back. Sonny's giving you his note:

'Well, read it then.'

'Hold on.' One last word.

'Mine first, seeing as mine was done first. Then yours.' Sonny is always six months older.

Finished.

As it's your house, you get to hold his completely blank sheet of paper up to the electric fire.

'Well?' He's leaning so close he's almost pushing you into the bars.

You push back: 'Give it time. The label said two minutes. We've hardly had two seconds yet.'

If you make the message work, then maybe the drowning won't happen tonight. You must hold the paper as near the heat as you can.

'You'll burn it.'

Sonny's snatched his paper and started waving it from side to side, flapping it away from the heat. Useless. You're going to drown.

Grabbing him by the wrist, you push his hand right up to the electric bars.

'Hey!'

You hold him firm. This time it's got to work.

'That's hot!' He drops the sheet and blows on his fingers. The paper's gone very dry and parchmenty and there's faint pink lettering.

'D...I...M...P—'

The gang's 'Dim Poko, Eager Bread' password, but the letters are already fading. You're going to drown.

Sonny gives the proper response by leaning close and chucking himself under the chin:

'Eager Chin! Eager Chin!'

'Dim Poko, Dim Poko,' you reply automatically. What does it matter anyway? The drowning will soon begin. Stupid passwords will change nothing.

'Come on, Malcolm. Eager Chin! Eager Chin!'

Sonny is standing at the other side of the room.

'Dim Poko, Dim Poko.' Have you managed to answer out loud? He's staring at you. Maybe you said something else? You want to shout 'Help! Help!'

Slowly, heavily, you get to your feet. Nothing will stop the drowning seeping into your room. Deeper and deeper until it covers you, until you can't move. Until you can't breathe.

'What about the Lego?' Sonny suggests.

You shrug. He knows where it is. You watch him build a frame, first using only the blue and white pieces, then locking the rest together like a box. He starts driving one of the cars in and out of a gap in the front wall. There's no petrol pumps because this is to be a proper works garage, he's explained. He pulls the wheels off a lorry and repairs it, then crashes it into some parked cars.

Your dad once showed you how to load up the lorry with marbles to make it into a bomber plane. He's talking to you now from Mission Control:

'Approaching target. Bandits at five o'clock.'

Your rear-gunner *bam-ham-bams* them out of the sky.

'Maintain altitude. Ten degrees west.' Your dad's voice is guiding you, telling you when exactly to open the tail-flap and shake the lorry, scattering marbles in every direction. 'Three, two, one — and bombs away!'

A direct hit.

'Mission accomplished. Return to base.'

The lorry crash-lands on the runway and skids full-length onto its side. You've survived, but where has your dad's voice gone? Listen as hard as you can:

Sonny's screaming out the ambulance sirens and fire-engines.

Listen harder:

The drowning-silence, coming nearer.

You begin to roll marbles at the lorry to knock it flat. Three times you take aim, and miss. Your fourth misses as well.

You hurl the rest in one large fistful. You're trying to break the room, to see it crack across like glass. Marbles hit the wardrobe and the chest of drawers full-force, making a great clatter against the woodwork. Then they bounce all over the place, harmlessly. What's the use of that?

You stay as you are, kneeling on the carpet and staring straight ahead at nothing.

'I brought some bits of my dad's old Meccano as well,' begins Sonny. 'My dad—'

Sonny's dad. Who cares about Sonny's dad? You glare at him, grab him, shove him to the floor. You pin his arms down with your knees. Who wants to hear about his dad? What does *he* matter? You press your knees down harder. To force him to be still. To shut him up. As you push down you can see yourself reflected in Sonny's eyes: clear as in the mirror, but shaped wrong. As if it was you being pressed and squeezed.

How tired you are suddenly. Letting go, you roll over and go completely limp. Peaceful, almost.

A deep breath of the dust-and-feathery smell under the chair. So peaceful. Why can't it always stay like this? You and Sonny, playing in front of the fire with the carpet solid under you, and no silence to come; no drowning?

Lying the way you are, you see the room like it's standing on its edge: what was the floor is now one of the side walls, carpeted and with furniture sticking out into space. The new floor's below you, it's wallpapered — and if the curtains were pulled they'd hide the window underneath like the bear-traps used by cavemen. You'll have to hold tight onto the carpet or else you'll fall downwards out through the window and right off the face of the earth into outer space. Sonny looks funny sticking out of the wall, like a flagpole gone wrong. Really stupid.

You sit up:

'Dim Poko! Dim Poko!'

'What—?'

You start chucking him under the chin:

'Eager Chin! Eager Chin!'

No response. What's wrong with him?

Then, leaning really close, your lips almost touching his, you hiss, 'Eager Chin!' and chin him really hard.

He's backed away slightly, but you keep step with him and will keep chinning him until he answers.

'Eager Bread!'

'Eager Chin!'

'Dim Poko! Dim Poko!' you both shout and begin chasing each other round the room, thrusting your faces close together and calling out at the tops of your voices. Faster and faster you go: you chin him and he chins you; you chase, he chases. Round the room, into the corner, round the chair. You won't stop, and you won't let him stop. You're banging into the furniture, slamming into the wardrobe and being bounced off it onto the tea chest, the corner of the bed—

You must keep going until you reach what happens next.

'Dim Poko! Dim Poko!' Your voice getting hoarse and sore—

Crashing into the wall, the fireplace, the wardrobe—

Keep going until… until…

You grab one of his dad's precious Meccano pieces and begin bending it. Keep bending it until the metal buckles in two. Then drop it onto the carpet. Another piece.

'Stop it, eh!'

It's almost giving—

'I said stop it.' Sonny's trying to prise your fingers apart. You mustn't let go. The edge of the metal's cutting into your palm. He's forcing your hand slowly backwards until it's almost breaking.

You can give in now: the Meccano's buckled to nothing and most of the green paint's flaked off, leaving raw metal.

'What are you playing at?'

You glare back at him:

'What do you know?'

'What do you mean? Look what you've done.' He's sticking his dad's stupid Meccano piece in your face. 'It's ruined.'

'What do you know? What do you know?'

'What are you on about, Malcolm?'

'Everything. That's what I'm on about. Everything.' Your voice sounds like the metal's still being twisted inside you. A good kick, and the pile of Meccano gets scattered across the floor.

'And what's everything?'

'Nothing to you anyway. You know nothing about it. Nobody does.'

A few minutes later Sonny's left, taking his dad's Meccano. Who needs it anyway? Or him?

The twisting hurts. You've sat too close to the fire and are almost burning. You don't move.

Your mother comes in. She's been crying again. Tea will be ready in five minutes, she says.

You don't answer. Why should you? You continue staring into the fire.

'Is everything all right? I thought Sonny was still here.'

You nod without looking up.

She's about to touch you. You mustn't let her. If you can make her cry again, the twisting inside you will stop. You could have her in tears, making her plead, beg. The twisting's cutting deeper into you.

Get to your feet before she comes any nearer — tell her you'll be through in a moment.

She's gone. You're five minutes nearer drowning.

Maybe if you close the curtains you'll shut out the dark water.

Out of the window you can see the low road going up to the village cross, the dyke and the Hendersons' garden. All the rest must be sky. When your light's switched off, everything will vanish and there'll be only dark water. So you must close the curtains.

Left side. You reach up, take the dark blue material in your hand.

If this was a real day you'd be in the kitchen listening for the Transit, waiting to see it coming over the hill. It brakes at the village cross, then there's the split-second's vanishing of the red tail-lights as your dad comes round the back of the van. If you shut the curtains now you will shut out everything that's ever happened — is that what you want?

Wait, don't go straight into the kitchen. Your mother's already started laying the table — for *three* places. See, she's put down a plate where your dad used to sit. Has she forgotten? Now she's standing quite still, her fingers tracing the outside rim of the plate. Making a circle once, then again. Dad always sat down first, but for the last few months there's just been the two of you. She's picked the plate up and is holding it flat against her chest. If you wait a few minutes longer she might even smash it. Her eyes are wavery. What will you do if she starts crying? Hold her? Tell her you're the man of the house now, and you'll look after her?

As quietly as possible you turn and go back to your room. You stand at the window. The snow-covered garden and fields are like a secret message still to be read. A perfectly blank sheet of paper with black trees, telegraph poles and hedges where it's become torn.

8

It was too early for Fiona to visit Mrs Goldfire's room. She would wait. She would unpack, check up on any business matters that had arisen during her absence, have dinner, then read. She was in complete control. When she felt ready, then she would go upstairs. This time there would be no temptation, no desire — just closeness, forgiveness.

Stella and Cook were having late afternoon coffee when she went into the kitchen. The moment she entered they fell silent.

'Good afternoon, ladies.'

'Good afternoon, Miss McBride.'

They asked her about the funeral. She told them. Then they fell silent again.

'Is everything all right, ladies?'

Stella nodded.

Cook prompted her:

'You should tell her, Stella. Go on.'

'Well, I really should have mentioned it at the time, but with your going off to a funeral and everything—'

'That's all right, Stella. I quite understand.'

'Well, it's really nothing, but when I went into one of the residents' rooms a day or two back—'

'One of the upstairs ones, you said,' interrupted Cook.

'Yes. Top landing. Well, I went in with the breakfast and, something really odd, all the photographs were turned face down.'

'I don't understand.' Had she spoken in a normal voice? She rested her right hand against the door, steadying herself.

'The photos on the dresser, as if they'd fallen over. Queerest thing. It was top landing, like I said. Mrs Goldfire, poor old soul, can't even get out of bed, never mind start rearranging the furniture.'

'Funny thing to do, any road. All right herself, is she?' asked Cook, touching the side of her head.

'All right as they ever are. Doesn't know the day of the week, where she is, who she is — same as normal. But she must have got up and done it. Nobody else.'

Stella was looking at her. And Cook, too.

She had to say something.

'Beats everything, that.' Cook shook her head.

A deep breath. 'Yes, it seems most extraordinary.'

'Who'd touch the old biddy's photos? What for? Never out of her bed these last three years. Been no trouble at all. Then this.'

Could she manage to speak properly? The slightest pause, then:

'Did Mrs Goldfire seem to have noticed anything herself?'

'Notice anything? She'll not notice when she's dead, that one!'

Cook drew a sharp intake of breath, 'Stella!'

'But it's true. You don't see the half of it down here, Daisy. The ground floor's the fast-lane, with the mobiles zimming around on their frames. The top floor's different, poor souls — breaks your heart seeing them. You need a joke now and again to keep you going. Don't you, Miss McBride?'

There was a silence for several seconds. Both women were still looking at her. She glanced beyond them to the window. Darkness was falling outside and she could hear the splash of rain against the glass. Cold rain that soaked through clothes, through skin itself.

Fiona closed the door behind her, stood for a moment perfectly still to breathe in the atmosphere of the room, then switched on the bed light. She could hardly wait now. She was in total control: downstairs lay the hall, her sitting-room, her office, the kitchen, the bedrooms and corridors.

'Rosehaven' — with her at the centre.

She glanced at the photographs on the dressing-table: the wedding, the bungalow, the group of children; then turned them over. They would have to be reset afterwards. She wouldn't forget twice. The perfume next, inhaling each scent deeply. She left the eau-de-Cologne until last; and all at once, within reach, was her mother's bedroom on that September morning.

She crossed to the bed and knelt down. It wasn't temptation that had brought her here. Nor wickedness. Not this time. She had struggled and at last found peace. Never had she felt so pure, so filled with grace. Never had she felt herself approaching so near God's presence.

She lifted Mrs Goldfire's hand from her head and laid it on the covers. The old lady's fingers looked so very frail — a careless touch might shatter the thin bones. When Mother was confined to bed during her last year she had often thought of ways to hurt her, and could have snapped each finger like a twig if she'd wanted. She stroked the open palm along the heartline, then the lifeline. She kissed them each in turn, then leant forward and kissed the old lady on the forehead. Such paper-dry skin, pale in the weak light. Every muscle slack and fleshy, the mouth drawn inwards as if life itself were already bitter-tasting. Her fingers stroked the old lady's cheek. Soon they would come to that moment of forgiveness and peace: as if their two lives reached into the very heart of what was theirs alone, to find not anger, not fear — but joy.

When she was a little girl she'd loved breathing onto her bedroom mirror, then tracing the outline of her hair, her cheeks, her eyes, until gradually her own face appeared smiling at her once more. By themselves her fingers had already started doing the same on the old woman's hair, her forehead, the bridge of her nose, her mouth. How well she knew that face now.

Tenderness and love were flowing through her. Again she leant forward to kiss Mrs Goldfire's brow. How comforted the old lady looked. A lightness had come into her eyes, the lines seemed smoothed, her mouth smiling almost.

A stranger seeing the two of them together would be aware only of a commonplace affection, as between mother and daughter. They would observe but not understand how truly miraculous this was. She could feel tears starting down her cheeks. Not from sadness, though. These were the proofs of true feeling. If she went to the mirror now she would see herself tear-stained, but radiant. Free, at last, to show her love.

Mother was near. She could feel her in the clasp of the old woman's hands, in the smell of her skin. The days of exhausting work, the evenings spent anxious and alone, the nights that had been blanked out: these had happened to someone else, not to her. She understood so much now. She understood how—

'Have you no strength, girl?' Mother's voice.

She froze.

The old lady's hands were beating jerkily against the top sheet, she was moaning and seemed to be trying to turn her head to one side. Her face was completely covered by the pillow.

She was pressing it down.

'Mother, Mother.' The muscles of her arms had set rigid.

She could feel the tears flowing down her cheeks, into her mouth. A saltiness she could almost bite on. 'Mother.'

All at once she's managed to jerk herself free, and stands panting beside the bed. She lifts the pillow, but will not look underneath. Whether the old woman is dead or not will change nothing:

- Not the streetlight slanting across the far wall.
- Not the chest of drawers bulking the darkness to her right.
- Not the framed picture above the bed.
- Not the silence from the street outside.

For her, there is nothing, nothing else. She is alone.

She listens. There are no footsteps coming along the corridor; there is no one standing behind her. She stands up. She's trying to stop her arms shaking. Trying to hold herself firm. Trying to put the photographs back. The frames rattle against the hard wooden surface. She nearly drops one. The room is stifling hot. She's trying to stop shivering.

The old lady remains insensible on the bed: her eyes closed, her hands motionless on the covers.

Turning, Fiona stumbles into the darkness of the corridor.

II

Darkness

9

Pausing before she takes the next stair, Fiona *tap-tap-taps* her fingers on the banisters. If only Margaret hadn't arrived she'd be getting on with her work; her whole routine will be in chaos now. She should be at her desk attending to her correspondence, then having a quiet dinner before an evening in front of the fire. She really does care for her sister and for Malcolm, of course, but...

It's nearly a month since she visited Mrs Goldfire, nearly a month that she's managed to resist temptation. Every single night has been a struggle: picturing the old woman's room, imagining the touch of her hand and the sense of release that would come flooding into her. Since running from the room there has been no peace, no rest, not even for one moment. Only the flames, and her terror of what will come after them.

She will have to raise her voice for her sister to hear on the landing above:

'You're back in your old room, Margaret.'

Then firmly grip the banisters and carry on up.

'That's good, Fiona. You've kept the stained-glass window. They're coming back into fashion at the moment. And Granny's old bowl, I'd forgotten that.'

Margaret has pointed out the window. Malcolm's response:

'Makes the place look gloomy. Like a church.'

'Ssh!'

'Come on, Mum. Get a move on.' He's bounding up the stairs two at a time and back down again, his shoes thumping the carpeted tread, then clattering on the polished edge. He's humming 'The Grand Old Duke of York' and at any moment will probably start singing out loud. She should tell him to be quiet, but surely that's his mother's job. On their first day, certainly.

'You're going to wear yourself out, son.'

'No, I won't. Just watch. Look, Mum! There's a chair here that'll go up and down the stairs like a ski lift. Easy as anything.'

High time to say something:

'That chair-lift is locked and remains locked unless I say so. It's for the residents.'

Margaret's taken the hint at last and grabbed him by the shoulder:

'Just slow down when I tell you. There's other people living in the house. They need peace and quiet.'

And one makes eighteen, and one makes nineteen and both feet twenty. That's how she used to climb the stairs before little sister Margaret came along, and the room was still hers. Counting the pattern, she'd called it, and the shape that the numbers made in her head followed the steps' rising sweep to the top landing. Her room had been halfway between two floors, not really on a landing of its own, at number twenty-eight.

'You dancing, Aunt Fiona?'

Without meaning to she must have again begun climbing the colours, following them from side to side on their way up the carpet. A green stretch is the next piece of solid ground, large and welcoming on the step above. If she places her foot in the middle of it, then no part of her will be left unprotected, and she can stay there for several seconds completely at ease. Completely safe.

What nonsense. There's no need for colours any more, or counting. She has her routine. Her days and nights are fully accounted for, in advance.

'I've no spare room ready at the moment, I'm afraid, so Malcolm will have to share with you tonight. I put in an extra bed so you should be all right.'

'We'll be fine, thanks. Nice of you to keep it for us, Fiona.'

Twenty-six, twenty-seven, twenty-eight and safe. That's what she used to say as she slammed the door shut behind her.

Her room until she was twelve and was moved upstairs. Different curtains now, different bedspread, the chest of drawers in a different place; but still with its dormer window and old-fashioned lock on the door. The wallpaper has been painted over, there's a fitted carpet, light-coloured. Her sister had the place littered with dolls, animals, shells, fluffy-eared donkeys, grubby-looking feathers and pebbles spilling everywhere. For herself, she'd always kept the room neat and clean, to feel the grain of the shiny woodwork under her fingers, and to see out of the window.

'Do you know what happened to my stuff when I left? My dolls and everything?'

'I've no idea.' Mother, of course, had burned them. No sense in upsetting Margaret by telling her. She'd be tactful:

'Didn't you take them with you?'

'The way I left? I grabbed some clothes, a towel and that was about it, if you remember. Pity about the dolls, I thought of coming back for them later.'

'If I'd known—'

'It would have been too late. Straight into the bin with the lot, if I know our mother. She'd have loved doing it, too.'

Having put down her suitcase, Margaret's gone over to the window:

'The garden's hardly changed. The lilac tree, the roses, the old shed still falling apart.' She laughs.

She'll cross over to stand beside her; maybe things won't be too difficult between them.

The pane is clouded with condensation, making the view outside seem a little distanced. Not good for the woodwork either.

With one quick movement Margaret's rubbed the window clear:

'Remember how the kids climbed the walls and ran into each other's gardens? Much easier than going the long way round.' Her sister starts pointing out the different trees to Malcolm.

Through the gap in the conversation she can see a clear winter's sky without clouds — like a perfect summer's day, but the deepest ice-blue. Long shadows stretch away from the house, the roof reaches beyond the lawn to the far wall, with its chimney pots slanting even further. It must be nearly twenty years since Margaret lived in the house; no wonder she seems tense — best to try a lighter touch to make her feel welcome:

'You in your old room here, and me upstairs! Just like old times!'

'Old times?' Margaret's turned to her and laughed. 'Let's hope not!' She should laugh in response.

She has managed a smile, and, without really knowing why, she touches Margaret on the arm.

Her sister's looking at her as if expecting her to say something. The weather?

'You've brought good weather with you. So far it's been raining for days. Weeks.' She should say something else. 'Cold drizzly rain that makes everything feel closed in.' Her fingers are still on Margaret's arm. If Malcolm wasn't there she might take her hand. To comfort her. Yes, that's why she's touched her, why she is talking so much: she wants to comfort her sister in her sad loss. At least Margaret isn't being tearful; it was over a month ago now. 'I mean, it's good to have you here again. Both of you.' An encouraging smile. 'We'll have tea downstairs, when you're ready.' Another smile. 'Lemonade for you, Malcolm, if you prefer.'

'I like Coke. Lemonade's—'

Margaret has glared him into silence. 'We'll be down shortly, Fiona. Thanks for everything. It's a lovely surprise to have my old room again. Really.'

'Ten minutes then?'

'We'll be down.'

She leaves, closing the door behind her.

The door-handle releasing itself into place: that was when she used to feel sanctuary slipping from her. When she stood with her forehead pressed against the door panel, waiting for as long as she could before turning round to begin her journey downstairs. The entire house is directly behind her: the rooms that had obeyed Mother's voice, the staircase that curved to the tone she spoke in. It had been a dream-house: another woman's house, another woman's dream.

'Lemonade's boring.' Malcolm's whine comes through the closed door.

Margaret hushes him:

'Ssh!'

Nothing to be afraid of nowadays, of course. Fiona lets go the handle and begins making her way downstairs. Surely her sister was joking when she said stained-glass was coming back into fashion. None of the angels clustering around the text look the least bit fashionable. Mother had had the window put in as 'a daily reminder of God's eternal Presence'. From when she could first read she'd spelt out the lettering every day: FEAR GOD IN LIFE, changing the emphasis on the separate words, trying to make it less harsh. Without success. She'd tried changing the order: FEAR LIFE IN GOD, but it seemed to mean much the same. She'd grown to hate those words. Then one day, it must have been in summer as the sunlight was so strong, the colours of the entire window — angels, scrolled decoration and message — lay clear and backwards-readable on the stair carpet, like mirror-writing. At once, she'd trampled them underfoot. She jumped on the four words in turn. Then again, and each time she thumped both feet on the step she said a swear-word: 'Hell', 'Damn', 'Bloody'. Knowing only three swear-words she had to repeat, 'Hell', which sounded the worst. Next she climbed to the step above to jump on them from a greater height and with her full weight. Then two steps above, then three, then four and jumping harder each time. It was a wonder she hadn't gone tumbling down the stairs. She'd turned to go back up for one final spectacular five-step jump — and saw Mother staring down at her:

'Don't mind me, Fiona. Please carry on.'

She stopped and waited. There was bound to be a row — for making a noise, for damaging the woodwork, the paintwork, the carpet or even the sunlight itself. There had to be a row for something. But Mother had remained standing with one hand on the banisters watching in silence. She looked at her for a moment, then began counting her way back up the four steps. She was about to jump when Mother's voice came from above:

'Not going to try five this time?'

Rocking backwards on her toes to stop herself, she'd said nothing.

'Scared, Fiona? It's only one more step. Go on.' Mother had sounded excited.

'Did you never feel like smashing that bloody window?' Margaret's come down the stairs. 'Just picking up Granny's bowl and — crash!'

'Of course not. Mother would have—'

'What could she have done worse than she'd already done? Imagine it, Fiona, that window smashed to nothing!'

Her sister's picked up the brass bowl:

'Not so heavy either, but heavy enough.'

'Margaret! You're joking!'

She's pulled back her arm, taking aim:

'Do you think so?'

'Stop it! Stop it at once!'

Without putting down the bowl Margaret's turned to her:

'You sound just like her.' She's not smiling. 'Bitch that she was. Let's do it together. Let's do it now.'

Evidently she will still have to be the elder sister so, hand outstretched and adopting a firm tone of voice:

'Give me the bowl, Margaret.'

'You want to do it all by yourself?'

'Give me the bowl.'

'Still on her side, eh?'

'The bowl, please. What would a broken window change?'

'The air, maybe?'

'Don't be flippant.' She takes charge of the bowl. 'You were joking, weren't you?'

'Was I?' Margaret seems uncertain. 'Every time I walked past this window I thought of smashing it. And didn't.' She gives a shrug and carries on down the stairs. 'So I suppose nothing much changes!'

It would have been vandalism pure and simple. That was her little sister all over, still behaving like a child. Good job one of them at least had grown up. Should she remove the bowl altogether and so keep Margaret from temptation? Not to mention the inconvenience it would cause, and the cost.

No. She will show that she trusts her to behave properly. She will replace it on the same spot on the stair. Whatever happens will be between Margaret and her conscience.

If the window remains intact, if the bowl stays where it is, if everything in the house — even the flames burning her — remains the same, then she will survive. In time, hell too becomes familiar, a routine of days and nights.

Tonight she must take three pills, then be in bed by ten-thirty and fast asleep by ten-forty. She mustn't let Margaret keep her up late, talking. It's eight-thirty — best of all would be for her sister to go to bed now and have an early night, which would leave her free to carry on from where Malcolm came to his sudden halt in The Book of Ruth; which would be near enough to her normal routine. Instead, she's being forced to follow their voices and the thump-thump of their feet on the stairs, every step of the way to their room. A terrible racket, but she will make allowances as this is their first night. Margaret needs her, and she will not be found wanting. She will be strong.

Having looped in the black ribbon page-marker she lays the Bible down. It was a good idea to have Malcolm read to her after they'd had supper, and he can continue reading the following day at the same point — good training for him to find the place exactly. Having just lost his father... much of his training will be lost also. She will do all she can to be of help.

Five minutes should be enough for her sister to put Malcolm to bed, during which time she will make a pot of tea. It is as well she has such wide experience in giving words of comfort. Margaret cries easily. As a girl she'd cried at everything and nothing. She'd bring home a thrush with a broken wing and be too tearful to do anything in case she hurt it. Fiona herself ended up having to bind up the wing and look after her sister as well. She did that because she loved her.

Now, exactly what kind of tea will be most appropriate? Earl Grey? Lapsang Souchong? Darjeeling? Margaret still appears quite distressed, so perhaps the Lapsang is just a touch too exquisite, too different a taste. On the other hand, it might serve as a temporary distraction to get the two of them over those awkward first moments until they are ready to discuss her sad loss. But then, being so specifically exquisite, it does tend to define the occasion and to assert its own particular atmosphere at every sip, which is not at all the intention. Loss, once stated, should be speedily dispatched. The Earl

Grey can be similarly discounted: each scented mouthful, insisting 'Earl Grey' every few moments, will certainly interrupt any tête-à-tête intimacy by its suggestion of the presence of a third party. A pity, as she's very fond of it; its distinctive taste almost a companion when she takes tea alone. No, she must be strong; her own preferences will have to take second place. Darjeeling has character yet can be trusted to remain unobtrusive. So, Darjeeling it is.

The tea made, the cups and saucers carried into her sitting-room, she sits down. Her sister's taking a long time getting Malcolm settled; the sooner he feels at home the better. It will not do for a young boy of his age to miss too much school — had it been the holidays there would have been no problem. A glance at the clock, at the door, at the tea things. She will wait.

An hour later the two of them are sitting together, and Margaret, naturally enough, is in tears. Once again she's insisted on telling her how Peter had been found, how the doctor said he was recovering, how they hoped he'd be getting up for his dinner that day, what the most recent tests had shown. The whole distressing business. When her sister begins to cry, her words become increasingly unclear. She seems unable to stop going over and over the same details, which only makes her cry more. Next of kin are never allowed here normally, but even in her office they rarely cry. She escorts them to the deceased's room and discreetly withdraws, closing the door after her; and they never return to her office until they've made themselves presentable. That's when she offers them tea and words of sympathy, before they leave. This is a different situation, of course, but there can be no doubt that Margaret is making things harder for herself.

She's reached over to touch the back of her sister's hand, saying she'll pray for her. Margaret makes no reply. Her sister has never really understood prayer. She'd prayed for a rabbit once, then a bicycle, and even for a little sister of her own — when she was young. Probably she prayed for a husband too. Well, that prayer was answered.

'You must have seen it when we packed away Peter's stuff: the emptiness on his side of the wardrobe? That's what it feels like inside me, Fiona. He's still with me, and he's *not*.'

'Margaret, I know such a sad loss is hard to understand but—'

'I'm not talking about understanding. I don't want to understand. 'Peter's still with me and, at the same time, he's not. He's not.'

Her sister's voice is getting a little too loud.

A drop of milk into each of their cups, then dividing what tea remains in the pot. Pity there are no biscuits left.

'For me he only died a minute ago—'

A well-timed paper handkerchief. 'Here, Margaret.'

'—and the doctor said he was getting better. There was no secondary cancer. None. He was getting better.'

Best to let her get it off her chest. Fiona takes her sister's hand and gives it a squeeze whenever encouragement seems to be needed. She watches her tears, listens to the break in her voice. An elder sister's sympathy:

'You can stay here for as long as you want, of course. You know that.'

Time for a fresh tissue. She pulls one from the box. Plenty left, thank goodness.

The used handkerchief lies sodden and ragged on the shiny table between them; it is safe enough there for the moment.

'I'm sorry to make such a scene, but everything's just – just fallen apart. My husband, my home… my whole life, except for Malcolm, gone in less than a month.'

'Not everything, Margaret.' A sincere smile. 'And you have a home here, remember. We'll give Malcolm a room of his own tomorrow.'

'Thank you. But it's not…' she pauses. 'I'd better go to bed soon, if you don't mind. I'm very tired.'

They wish each other a good night, and Margaret leaves. Now she can pick up the handkerchief. It is still damp. She holds it tight, then brings it slowly up to her lips. The smell of her sister's tears.

Tick-tick-tick, Tick-tick-tick, Tick-tick-tick—
 You will drown, You will drown, You will drown.
 Your father's alarm clock beside you:
 Tick-tick-tick, Tick-tick-tick, Tick-tick-tick—
 You will drown in this house.
 You will drown in this room.
 You will drown in the dark.
 You will drown, you will drown, you will drown.
 Tick-tick-tick, Tick-tick-tick, Tick-tick-tick—
 You will drown in this room that says NO.
 In this house that says NO.

In this place that's said NO — NO — NO from the moment you stepped out of the train into the loudspeaker boom of Waverley station. The air was a choking blue of diesel smoke and burnt oil. Without looking around or waiting for you, your mother set off marching straight ahead. You had to follow at a half-run until you caught up, first at one side, then at the other. Bumping into the big blue suitcase, then into the black one.

 'Quickly, Malcolm, or we'll be here all day.'

 A horn behind you: a luggage trolley wanted to pass. The driver, a man with a fierce red beard, scowled at you.

 Your mother was already several steps further on. You hurried after her. The horn blared again.

 Bumping one of your plastic bags into her blue suitcase.

 'Watch, Malcolm!'

In front of you, beside you, behind you: hurrying men, hurrying women. You turned a corner:

'Look, Mum! There's a pigeon!'

A pigeon was pecking at a Pizza Hut box while people almost stepped on it.

'Deaf, are you?' The fierce red beard passed with its trolley, still scowling hard.

The pigeon rose with impossible suddenness into the air to soar above the trolleys, people and suitcases. Flapping its wings only twice, it passed within range of the booming loudspeaker, within range of being shredded by the distorted voice. Then, having drifted down unharmed in one smooth unbroken curve, it settled next to a rubbish bin and immediately began strutting towards some crumpled paper.

'Malcolm!'

She was at the end of a long line of people who had all just shuffled one step forwards.

'We stand here.'

Black taxis moving slowly, bumper to bumper, kept on coming from round the corner. You stopped counting after seventeen. The taxis in one queue, the people in the other. Two lines meeting exactly in the middle and getting paired off. No chance here to make the *outside* happen as it should. Even if you'd counted the people in the queue, you couldn't tell which would be *your* taxi. Sometimes two or three passengers got in at once. You were far down the queue, but the taxis kept on coming. There couldn't be so many.

'What if they run out?'

She wasn't listening. Just staring straight ahead, with the two suitcases at her feet which she slid a little forward every time the queue moved on. People went past, sometimes cutting between you to cross to their platform. Hardly anybody spoke. At your back a pair of glass doors swished open and closed like in *Space Precinct*.

'Are they electronic?'

Your mother had slid one of the cases too hard, making it topple over. She righted it, glared at nothing, then kicked it one place nearer the head of the queue. A taxi door slammed. Eleven people to go. The shop opposite didn't have any doors. The customers just walked straight in, rushed along the shelves grabbing newspapers and sweets, then joined a big queue circling the cashdesk. The woman was like an old-fashioned wind-up toy with candy-floss hair. Her hand jerked out once for the money, once for the change. Money, change; money, change.

And the queue-circle kept turning.

Your mother was speaking:

'—don't you think? I'm her only sister, after all. A taxi'd be easier all round,' she said. 'Easier for her.'

'I've never been in a taxi.'

'That's not the point.'

A hardness in her eyes, like Aunt Fiona. But when her hand touched your shoulder, to keep you moving forward, it wasn't a digging hand.

Your taxi was next. You climbed into the back, your mother gave the driver an address, and he moved off.

Into more noise, traffic, taxis screeching; lights cutting off and on like the real cities on TV. Your taxi stopped-and-started its way up a street of shops with pop-music blasting out. An ambulance with its siren screaming raced past on the wrong side of the road and went through a set of red lights. The driver said something you couldn't hear. Your mother answered, 'Right enough,' but she didn't really seem to be listening to him. Your taxi moved off again. The further you went from the centre of Edinburgh, the less city-like it seemed.

Finally you turned into an almost empty street. No traffic, no shops; no pedestrians, even. Just a line of big stone houses on each side, like cottages stuck on top of each other. It's the city, so they should have been skyscrapers or something exciting. The houses had numbers, not names. You stopped outside number twenty-three.

From your very first look the house said NO.

The unpainted stone walls said NO.

The dark windows said NO.

The flattened gravel path said NO.

The shut gate and the low wall with sharpened railings said NO.

Your mother didn't look at you, or move to pick up the suitcases. She was standing quite still.

'Mum, why do we have to stay with Aunt Fiona?'

She turned to you; she wasn't smiling:

'You don't want to, I don't want to. But we've no money, so we've no choice.'

She touched your shoulder. Then, not really... asking you, not even looking at you:

'Come on, son.'

Tick-tick-tick, Tick-tick-tick, Tick-tick-tick—

You will drown, You will drown, You will drown.

Your aunt's house is NO, Aunt Fiona is NO.

Tick-tick-tick, Tick-tick-tick, Tick-tick-tick—

The corridors, the stairs and the darkness are NO.

Whatever she says, your aunt's voice says NO.

NO — NO — NO, as you followed your mother into the hall after eating, and had to watch her go upstairs to finish the unpacking. The hall seemed made of dark wood, dark furniture and darkness. There was no curtain for the church-looking window. After she'd turned the stair at the first floor she was out of sight. The grandfather clock counted off six slow seconds, then you heard the bedroom door being closed. Another six seconds were counted off. That should have been when you explored the house; quiet with no one about. That's what should have come next but, in this house, it doesn't happen like that. In this house, even if you tell it differently, it doesn't stay different. Not with Aunt Fiona there. In these rooms and corridors the *outside* belongs to her.

'This is an historic house.' Aunt Fiona was standing behind you.

'Oh.'

The red-and-black carpet, the mouldy-looking tapestry like an old rug with holes in it hanging on the wall, the window made up of dark bits of glass, the staircase coming to a stop at the unlighted landing above — she wanted you to say you liked it.

You did your best:

'It must be really…ancient.'

Then she started on a list of dates and old relatives. The clock kept ticking and the wooden floor seemed to get harder.

'Shall we go into my private sitting-room?' She opened one of the doors, and you followed her in.

It was warmer and a little brighter, with a reading lamp shining on a half-finished jigsaw. There was a switched-off TV.

Once she had sat down in the chair in front of the gas fire, she asked:

'Are you looking after your mother, at this time of family grief and tribulation?'

No one in the village had gas. In cities like Edinburgh there are sometimes huge gas explosions and whole houses are blown up, killing people, but Aunt Fiona didn't seem bothered. She turned to the jigsaw while carrying on with her questions:

'Are you your mother's strength and support? A comfort in her sorrow and loss?' She glanced up at you. She's strange, especially her eyes. All day they've never just looked at you, but always *into* you. They stare.

She was holding what seemed to be a piece of blue sky in her hand. What was the right answer supposed to be? The piece of sky trembled, then was tried here and there: close to a half-finished roof, next to a flag.

'But you'll be doing all you can, Malcolm, I'm sure.' She returned the piece to join the others still unplaced at the side of the picture. 'Won't you?'

'Yes.'

A short pause, then she was back to staring into you. What was the matter? What had you said wrong?

'Yes, Malcolm—?' Her tone of voice was like the teacher's at school. Her eyes staring even harder.

'Yes, Aunt Fiona.'

The right answer. She nodded slightly but said nothing. On the mantelpiece a clock ticked slowly. The piece of sky was picked up and examined again. There was the faintest hint of cloud along one edge, otherwise it was entirely blue. She tried placing it next to the roof, the tree, the roof again, then the flag.

'The sky's always the hardest.' She wasn't staring into you any longer, but into the space between unfinished clouds. Next she tried it above some railings. The jigsaw was the picture of a large building. Someone's country house, maybe, with what looked like a regiment of soldiers in front. An army barracks? A pretty boring jigsaw.

'Yes. Your mother needs you now. You're all she's got. Apart from me, of course.' She didn't once smile or even glance at you, but kept trying the same piece in the same series of places. Then suddenly she looked up:

'And you, too. Remember, if you need comfort, if you need someone to talk to. You know you can come to me.'

Maybe the white mark wasn't a cloud at all. It could just fit above the horse and rider in the corner, with the edge being a part of its bridle. That was it. You should have told her. You'd have been helping her, and she would have been pleased.

Abruptly she'd laid the piece to one side again.

'How many Commandments were given to Moses?' Her stare had started digging into you. 'On Mount Sinai?' Another dig. 'The Book of Exodus.'

'Like the Moses we did in school? And God?'

'Is there any other God, Malcolm? The Lord God who spoke to Moses through the Burning Bush.'

'Oh.'

'You must know your Commandments.'

Aunt Fiona wasn't wearing a ring, which meant she wasn't married. Your mother sometimes lets you play with her rings. The engagement ring's best. When you touch it, you love rubbing your finger between the smoothness of the metal and the sudden sharpness of the stones. She won't need it now — now she's no longer married. Maybe if you ask, she'll give it you.

'Thou shalt have no other gods before me.' Aunt Fiona's eyes were digging even deeper.

What were you supposed to say? The fire was getting so hot against your leg, you had to take a step away from it.

'I was roasting.'

But she'd continued looking at the exact spot where you'd been standing:

'Thou shalt have no other gods before me.' A long pause, then:

'Well? What comes next?'

The heat from the fire had caught up with you and you had to move again.

She tapped the chair with her finger. 'A restless spirit?'

What did that mean?

'Thou shalt not take the name of the Lord Thy God in vain.'

What did she want?

'Repeat. Thou shalt not take the name of the Lord Thy God in vain.'

The easy bit first:

'Thou shalt not…'

'Thou shalt not take the name—'

'The name.'

'Of the Lord Thy God—'

'Thy God.'

'In vain.'

The end:

'In vain.'

You couldn't believe it when she asked you to repeat the whole thing all over again. Some chance. Then she went through it word by word until you could say it properly. No idea what it meant, of course. But who cared?

Five Commandments later she stopped and told you to learn them for tomorrow. Then, if it was no trouble, you were to read aloud to her from the Bible:

'It will be an inspiration to us both.'

You picked up the heavy book, opened it at the black ribbon and started labouring your way from the top left-hand corner down the first column, pausing for breath at the end of every two lines:

'Now it came to pass in the days when the judges ruled that there was famine in the land and a certain man…'

'Not so fast, Malcolm. These are God's words, not man's. God does not rush His Word, He has all eternity before Him and within Him. Begin at verse eight, please.'

'And Naomi said unto her two daughters in law…'

She sat with her eyes closed and seemed to know the story by heart. Sometimes she had whispered the next word or phrase to herself before you reached it. Well, if she knew it as well as that, why did she need you? Why did she even need the book?

You carried on reading and gradually her whisperings became less and less. Once she'd been quiet for four verses you began reading slower, and softer. Then not at all.

She was sitting with her eyes shut. Fast asleep. If you put the book down quietly, and if the chair didn't creak—

So, gripping the armrest, beginning to raise yourself up. Slowly, slowly—

Her sudden stare:

'The Bible finished, is it?'

You continued reading.

You'd just started on another column when your mother came in to get you ready for bed. You shut the book in mid-sentence, said goodnight and left.

Tick-tick-tick, Tick-tick-tick, Tick-tick-tick—

Your father was staring and staring and staring.

Tick-tick-tick, Tick-tick-tick, Tick-tick-tick—

You reached out to touch him, to wake him.

The *crack* of his head.

Aunt Fiona is downstairs. So now you can make the *outside* your own again. Again you can say how things will happen:

You should sit up in bed as he did, your eyes staring wide open, not blinking.

Placing your pillow to make yourself exactly as he was—

Relax. That was only the noise of a train passing in the distance. So faint, until it's gone altogether.

You must keep still. Very, very still. The room is growing quieter except for the alarm clock's *tick-tick-tick* exactly the same as in his room.

The darkness is pressing around you. You can't breathe; you're having to force your chest in and out. If you can stay as perfectly still, as perfectly silent as he did, you will be safe. Not a muscle of your face moving. When you want to blink, you mustn't; or scratch the itch starting on the side of your nose, or the one on your knee. Make your muscles stiff, rigid. Your eyes have begun watering with the effort. Your hand's pressed against your heart to keep it beating.

Another train passing. You can rest against its *rattle-rattle, rattle-rattle* for a moment, then begin tensing yourself for the silence that will come after. Then…

Each breath is being sucked from the air, and pushed back out with all your strength. After each breath there's a stillness that seems to last longer and longer.

Will someone come into your room and call your name?

Will they come nearer; tap your shoulder to wake you?

Is that when you'll start falling to one side?

You must stare, stare hard. Don't blink.

You must grit your teeth to stay still. Dead still. You must clench your fists.

Staying dead still; dead still; dead — dead—

III

Night

11

She'd been up since six to make sure everything would be exactly as planned. Not that they'd notice, but that was hardly the point. She wasn't doing it for them. Things had to be right:

- Butter in rounded pats soft and wet from the warm roller, to be picked up by the butter-knife.
- Lump sugar, to be lifted by tongs, not fingers.
- The side knives set on wooden slats, each with its cut groove holding the blade.
- A choice of cream, milk or lemon.
- The teapot and strainer, the coffee pot, the hot-water pot, the hot-milk pot.
- The linen napkins rolled in their holders.
- A choice of marmalade, honey, apricot jam, strawberry jam, each in a porcelain-lidded jar, with separate spoon beside.
- A basket of warm rolls, two racks of fresh toast — brown and white.
- A choice of cereals: muesli or corn flakes.
- A lidded tureen of porridge.
- Three places set: main plate and cereal bowl, side plate. Cutlery.
- The lightest of cups and saucers.

Their first breakfast together: she would start as she meant to go on. Things would be done properly, not like her sister's mug-of-coffee-and-slice-of-toast-affair. The best-but-one set of china. A risk, but just this once — for its very delicacy would surely help suggest the correct tone. If the occasion did arise, she was prepared to remind them not to use both hands when raising their cups. Formality, or chaos: there was no middle road.

It was her sense of formality, of moral firmness — significantly enough, the words were almost an anagram — that had allowed her to visit Mrs Goldfire again last night. She'd put Margaret's handkerchief, still damp with tears, into the old lady's hand:

'See how sorry I am? Feel it.'

After the previous unfortunate visit, and the problems she'd had resetting the photographs, she'd been nervous of going. For over an hour she had knelt by the bedside holding the old woman's hand in hers, stroking her arm. Waiting, waiting for a sign of God's mercy and love, His presence, at least. It had been a test. She understood that now.

The table looked perfect. Margaret and Malcolm would have to fit themselves into its formality and so be strengthened to bear their difficulties. When they deigned to appear, that was. Where were they? Already eight-thirty, and they'd been told quarter past.

Borders Time, perhaps?

Being the perfect hostess, she would wait. She would say nothing, and wait. When they came in she'd be standing at the window, her back to the door. Then the perfect hostess: she would turn, smile graciously, greet them and invite them to be seated. She'd say nothing about their lateness.

Last night had been a test — had she passed? God was not so easily placated. This morning would be a further test of her faith and of herself. It was precisely the kind of rain she hated and feared most that was sweeping across the garden. The tests were surely a sign of His favour. Well, she was ready to show her complete trust and obedience. Who should be kept waiting: her family, or God?

Not even stopping to change into weather-proof clothes, for that would be part of the test, she turned away from the window and left the dining-room. She passed through her office and went out the French windows, then down the metal veranda steps and into the garden. She stood in the centre of the lawn. The wind was ice-hard, the rain almost sleet. If God was protecting her, nothing else mattered.

Not the rain, the cold and, most of all, not Mother. She had been taken away and burned years ago.

Mother's house. Three storeys of closed doors, corridors and misery. She wanted to spit defiantly on the ground in front of it, but had never learned how to. She could curtsey 'like a good girl', she could offer round biscuits like a 'perfect little lady'.

But not *spit*.

When there had been guests Mother's tone of voice had changed dramatically and the first time she heard its warmth and good humour she had run over and hugged her. Mother had stroked her hair, and laughed. At last she'd done something right. She climbed onto Mother's knee to kiss her. She forgave her everything. The visitors were saying what a pretty child she was and so well behaved, and Mother was agreeing. She could hardly believe her ears. This was heaven. She'd clung closer, rested her head, taken Mother's hand to play with. The grown-ups talked and she was allowed to remain on Mother's lap. The room was warm with a coal fire burning. All she wanted was to close her eyes and sink deeper into that loving warmth. The voices murmured around her and, feeling herself in danger of falling asleep — she hadn't wanted to lose one second of her new joy — she'd glanced over to her father and smiled, showing him how Mother had changed. He'd shaken his head and looked away.

At that moment the sitting-room door opened and everyone's attention was distracted by whoever was about to come in. That was when Mother pinched her and hissed under her breath:

'Get off my knee before I knock you off.'

From then on, when visitors called she curtseyed, passed round biscuits, then sat rigid by herself, trying not to hear the warmth and friendliness in Mother's voice.

Suddenly, standing there on the wet grass, she felt more completely alone than ever before: she was getting soaked to the skin, her slippers were sodden through. Lifting the drenched hair from her face she touched the dampness on her cheek: rain. It was only rain.

Ten minutes later, having dried herself and changed, she went into the dining-room. Her sister and Malcolm had already started their breakfast.

'Good morning. Sorry I seem a bit late on our first morning together. I went for a quick stroll. Rather ill-timed.' A laugh to put them at their ease. 'It's terrible weather outside so we probably won't be able to go anywhere this afternoon, I'm afraid.' She sat down.

Her little sister was ready to argue, of course:

'Perhaps it'll clear. The weather forecast said—'

'Have you looked out the window, Margaret? It won't clear. I'm sorry but there it is.' She poured herself some tea.

Then Malcolm started:

'But, Mum, what does the rain matter? We could go to the Zoo, maybe.'

'It'll be better another day, son. You wouldn't see much anyway — the animals'll be in their sheds because of the wet.'

'No, they won't. Not all of them.'

Poor Margaret. If Malcolm was going to start answering back like that, she should learn to be firmer. He needed to be told, then he would know. He needed his mother to be strong, now more than ever. Change of topic:

'Did you sleep well, Margaret?'

'Perfectly, thanks. Yourself?'

'I always have, thank goodness. Malcolm?' Best to bring him into the conversation, show him he could feel at home, even if he was too busy eating toast to answer.

'Mmm.'

'Your Aunt Fiona's wondering if you slept well. Malcolm?'

'Yes.' Munch, munch.

And the 'Thank you, Aunt Fiona'?

She'd say nothing this time. Better to let him feel settled. Instead, ever the diplomat, she lifted the teapot to offer refills.

'So what will you do? This is a busy morning for me, unfortunately. Church, naturally. And some paperwork before I can start getting ready. The monthly accounts. Just me and my computer.' Best to make light of her work-load, so as not to embarrass Margaret. 'If the weather clears up perhaps you can go somewhere this afternoon. In the meantime why not take Malcolm on a bus-tour of the city? See the sights.'

'Not the Zoo?'

She'd been speaking to her sister, but once again she would have to be the soul of tact:

'As your mother says, you wouldn't see many animals on a day like this. A bus tour would be just the thing. Just the ticket, in fact!' She could make jokes as well as anyone. Children liked jokes.

'I wanted to go to the Zoo.'

'You will, Malcolm. Tomorrow, maybe.' Margaret was taking a firm line at last. 'But your aunt's right: a tour of the city would be perfect. The Royal Mile. Princes Street. The Castle.'

'Is there dungeons?'

'I'm sure there are.'

And his grammar? But she'd say nothing. 'There's a gun, Malcolm, that goes off at one o'clock. An enormous cannon.' Boys liked guns.

'Would they let us into the dungeons, Mum?'

Having finished breakfast, the perfect-hostess-cum-diplomat stood up:

'Well, I'd better get to work.'

'Sure you can't come with us, Fiona?'

'I'm afraid not. I have Church, remember. And businesses don't run themselves.'

'I only asked. It would have been nice.'

A mock-martyr smile. 'See you at lunch. Have a pleasant morning, both of you.' A friendly exit, and she went across the hall to her office and closed the door.

Desk, filing cabinet, Chinese fire-screen; two easy chairs and a low table for visitors or next of kin. Work, work. For several seconds she remained standing with the door handle pressed into the small of her back. She leant against it. She had invited them, given them a room; was she expected to provide perfect weather as well?

She crossed over to the French windows. The rain was spattering onto the veranda, *pink-pink, pink-pink*. The ironwork was rusty. She let her head rest against the glass. Cold, not like the touch of Mrs Goldfire's hand. That's what she would feel like in time. Colder, even. The rain was being driven towards the house, towards her, chilling everything in its way. She wouldn't go to the old woman's room again. She'd no more strength for tests of faith, for struggles against temptation. All she wanted was a moment's real peace — was that too much to ask? By day she worked and worked herself to exhaustion, but as night approached God's love was never enough.

'Fiona?' Margaret had come into the room.

For a split-second she almost rushed towards her sister, but managed not to.

'Fiona? We've decided to go on the tour later, and wondered if you'd like to come.'

She watched the plants out on the terrace being drenched by the rain — the nearest had a pool of water round the base of its stem — then turned. 'We'll see. As I said, I've correspondence to deal with. Afterwards there's Church. Not everyone's on holiday, you know.'

'Holiday?'

'I'm sorry, Margaret. I wasn't thinking. Please forgive me.' She took a step away from the window.

'I meant in the afternoon.'

What was her sister talking about, 'the afternoon'? Another step. The coldness seemed to be coming nearer, even here.

'Are you all right, Fiona?'

'Yes, I'm fine. I'm sorry I seemed snappy at breakfast. I suppose I'm just not a breakfast person. Not used to conversation first thing in the morning. I improve as the day goes on.' A reassuring smile.

Then, out of nowhere, Margaret started on about Mother, saying she was worried about her and they should discuss her that evening. *Mother*, for goodness sake. Well, she'd nip that one in the bud. She picked up a few of the letters lying on the desk. 'We'll see.'

'We'll see? Really, Fiona, it would help a lot.'

'We'll see, I said.' A glance at the envelopes. With all the upset of their arrival the day before, she'd not had a chance to look through the mail. Electricity bill, a circular, probably from the Health Board.

'That's what Mum used to say when she meant "no".'

'Why do you keep going on about her? I don't want to discuss her. Not now, nor this evening either.'

'No one's asking you to. I'm worried about Malcolm, I said.'

'You said "Mum".'

'I did not. Fiona, are you sure you're all right?'

'Perfectly, thank you. Just very busy.' A meaningful smile. Her sister could deny it if she wanted to, but she had said 'Mum'.

'Is this you improving as the day goes on?'

Another smile, more relaxed:

'I'm trying to. It's that time of the month and I had a bad night. Usually I only have the staff to take it out on. Sorry.'

'Plenty of tea, remember.'

'Don't I just. My tiny little sister wearing out the carpet up to my bedroom bringing me cup after cup.'

'It made me feel grown up. Like I was taking part.'

'Well, the bills seem to appear at the same time, unfortunately! I'd better get on with them. Enjoy yourselves.'

By herself again she sat down at the desk to begin looking through the letters. She'd work and work, prepare herself for Church, then go to Church and come back home; have lunch, then work, then tea with Margaret and Malcolm, then a bath. Then dinner, then conversation, then bed at ten-thirty. The day was planned and her plan would be stuck to. She would grit her teeth and sit there at the window and work, and ignore the dampness seeping into the woodwork behind her, into the very glass.

Cold November rain.

Her sister was really the limit sometimes: forcing her to pretend about her period, or else Margaret would have kept on and on. Hardly in the door one day and already on about Mother, who'd died years ago; end of story.

She slit the first envelope. The electricity bill. She was writing out the cheque when the door opened.

Margaret came in carrying a cup of tea. Without a word she laid it on the desk, smiled and left.

Fiona continued writing the cheque, then folded it into the return envelope, which she placed in the out-tray. The teacup might mark the desk so she put a drug catalogue underneath it before going on to the next letter.

That chillness on the side of her face exposed to the window: from time to time she raised her free hand to protect her cheek.

12

Now that you've had breakfast and are away from Aunt Fiona you can say how things will happen: exploring the top floor comes next. You've been told to stay in all morning and not to make a noise. Fine. You've taken off your shoes and are sliding on the shiny wooden floor in your stocking-soles. You've not to slide down the banisters, not to go into any of the rooms; you've not to 'jump around'. You never jump around anyway, and certainly not here. Nobody does. The house is three floors, all of them saying NO and doing NO, except behind some of the doors — where you can hear TVs going, or a radio.

But not a sound, you've been told. No laughing, even if it's a comedy programme or joining in with the jingle. Not even clicking your fingers. These are Aunt Fiona's residents.

Downstairs was bad enough, with that church-looking window shutting out the daylight, but up here on the top storey's even drearier. A corridor of closed doors. Dark wood, dark walls; a fire-extinguisher at one end and nothing at the other, which leaves plenty of room for a full slide along the floor to the top of the stairs. Then looking over the banisters all the way down to the hall, like battlements on a castle. There are attackers swarming up, hundreds of them, and only you defending. But you've got them where you want them: they can only fight you one at a time, in hand-to-hand combat. They keep on coming and you keep beating them back, sliding from side to side on your stocking-soles.

You're defending Aunt Fiona's residents.

Silent sword-fights to the death, you never shout in triumph and they don't cry out as they tumble down into the moat. You're called the Silent Warrior. Even when you're battling with two of them at once — sliding, turning a quick circle to face the second man who's getting to his feet again — you keep a deadly silence. They're lying at your feet. You give each of them a kick that sends him rolling down to the next flight, and two more take their place. But the Silent Warrior has wiped his sword clean and is ready for them.

'What's this noise? Malcolm, come with me at once!' Aunt Fiona. Out of nowhere. Leaning too close to you. Her eyes stabbing at you; the damp crumbly smell of her face-powder.

'But, Aunt Fiona, I wasn't—'

'Don't argue, Malcolm. In here.' She has pushed open the nearest door, then, taking you by the shoulder, shoves you into the dirty-water smell of your dad's room.

You're not going in. It's dark but his eyes will be staring hard at you, and nothing will stop him from slipping to one side: his head will crack.

You grip the door-handle, and hold on.

She's pushing, she's telling you to let go, telling you to do what you're told. You have to keep her on the *outside*. If she makes you go into the room, you know what will happen next.

She's twisting your fingers back and shoving. Telling you, breathing hard at you: her hands are grabbing, forcing...

All at once you've stumbled forwards; your voice not even speaking loud, it's so clenched and stiff:

'No! No!'

The light is abruptly snapped on.

An old woman wrapped in a woollen shawl is lying in the bed. That's all. Nothing, no-one else: the *outside* is back where it belongs. Her skin looks grey, dirty white and reddish all at the same time. Her eyes are open, but she's snoring. Her crumpled bedcap has slipped to one side showing more bald bits than hair underneath. She must be a hundred years old.

Aunt Fiona glares at you:

'You were told not to disturb the residents. Weren't you?'

She wouldn't hit you, but her voice does. 'You were told (*smack*), weren't you' (*smack*). You feel the *stab-stab* of her eyes.

On a small side-table stands a snow-scene ornament, which, if you shake it, will make a blizzard round the piper trapped inside. Maybe if you made a snowstorm to cheer up the old woman Aunt Fiona wouldn't be so angry? Your dad would have liked seeing it.

'Mrs Goldfire (*smack*) is trying to rest (*smack*).'

It's so hot in the room. You're roasted too, after fighting and defending the residents. So hot you're feeling dizzy. If you pick the ornament up, with Aunt Fiona watching, you might end up dropping it. Then she'd get really mad. Better not.

She's bending down to straighten the old woman's cap. Even then, her eyes never leave you:

'Old people need rest. They don't need small boys running and shouting up and down the corridors. When your father was ill, I'm sure your mother didn't let you behave like that.'

'I was trying to be quiet.'

The right answer. Aunt Fiona seems to relax but only for an instant:

'Were you, indeed? Well, don't tell *me*. It's Mrs Goldfire you were disturbing. Tell *her*. And tell her how sorry you are.'

The old woman's not even looking at you. Her eyes are like your dad's were when you went into his room. They're pointed in your direction, but seeing somewhere else. If Aunt Fiona asks you to touch her, to get her attention, you'll run.

She's jerking her hand as a sign for you to move closer. Two steps, and now you can see teardrops gathered in the corners of the old woman's eyes.

Aunt Fiona's harsh whisper:

'You see what you've done? You see?'

But you couldn't have made her unhappy just by playing, could you?

Another jerk of Aunt Fiona's hand.

Another step closer: the old woman's crushed-looking face, the dullness of her wet eyes.

'What were you going to tell her? Come on, Malcolm. Speak up.'

You're not going any nearer.

'I was trying—'

Suddenly the old woman's head lolls heavily to one side, making the tears run down her cheeks.

You never even touched her, just started speaking. In a moment you are going to start crying. You must dig your fingernails into the palm of your hand to stop yourself; you must bite your lip. You're not going to cry, not for Aunt Fiona.

'I was trying to be quiet.'

'Louder, Malcolm. Mrs Goldfire is slightly hard of hearing.'

'I was trying to be quiet.' Then you stare down at the carpet.

'That's better.'

When you look up, her face is making a hard smile:

'Now, wouldn't you like to say how sorry you are? You'll feel so much better afterwards.' Another hard smile. 'And tell Mrs Goldfire you'll never do it again.'

Better if you could just go. But you can't. Any more than you could ever reach out and touch the old woman. You can't speak either. Aunt Fiona stops everything from happening as it should.

'She wants to forgive you, Malcolm.'

Staring back down at the carpet.

The door opens and someone comes in carrying a tray.

'Pardon me, Miss McBride, I didn't know you were here.'

'That's all right, Stella. Malcolm and I have finished. He's just getting to know some of the residents. Learning to keep himself out of mischief — eh, Malcolm?' A different smile this time, supposed to be friendly looking. 'Come on, then.'

The two of you go out of the room.

'As today is Sunday—' Aunt Fiona marches you down the stairs with her hand on your shoulder, 'I'll be leaving for Church in an hour. You can come with me. I know your mother is not a church-goer, but she could have no possible objection. Or you can stay in to learn the Ten Commandments.' The hard, hard smile. 'The choice is yours.'

'Can't I just go outside and play? We'll be going on that bus tour all afternoon.'

'It's Sunday. Malcolm. A day of rest. You have already demonstrated that playing is too noisy.'

'I can play at Stealth Bombers. They're silent.' You have reached your bedroom.

'The Ten Commandments, remember. Or you come to Church with me.' No smile this time.

13

Sunday meant nothing to her sister. To Malcolm, making that row upstairs, it meant nothing. To Stella and the other staff it meant nothing.

Fiona returned to her sitting-room and shut the door. Mother's Bible lay on the side table. Having switched on the gas fire and taken her seat, she picked up the book. 'Florence McBride', written in thick fountain-pen on the flyleaf. Mother had given it to her on the day she died. No longer strong enough to hold its weight, she had pointed to it. Had Mother really hoped she would read aloud to her? Some last words of comfort?

Today was God's day, not Mother's. The Bible was hers now. The house was hers. God would be hers again, in time. She opened the heavy volume on her lap. The Book of Ruth. Knowing every word by heart, she closed her eyes and placed her hands palm-down on the text to try drawing His strength from the very ink and paper of the book itself. God's Holy Word:

'And Ruth said: Intreat me not to leave thee, or to return from following after thee: for whither thou goest I will go; and where thou lodgest, I will lodge.'

If she was calmer, she would hear God speaking within her, spreading through her body, cleansing her, inspiring her… but she was so tired. A moment's true peace, and she would surely hear Him once more.

'Look at me, girl,' Mother had called from her bed. That pleading tone.

God had bid her say nothing.

'Daughter.' Her voice was splintering and already faint. 'Daughter, come to me.'

He would not let her move.

'Daughter?' A whisper. More breath than voice. 'Fiona?'

The force of God's Word no longer entered directly from the page through her outstretched palm, no longer made her dizzy with His power. His love. There was no peace any more...

In that room she had done only His bidding: she remained quite still. God was with her when she watched Mother die. Afterwards His first command had been for her to arrange the soonest cremation possible, not the burial Mother had wished. His second was for her to throw out everything, the Bible excepted: Mother's clothes, papers, letters, photographs. By the following morning no trace of Mother had remained. God commanded, and she had obeyed.

There was a knock at the door.

'Miss McBride?'

She closed the Bible and looked up to face the intrusion:

'Well, Stella? What is it that is so important?'

'I'm sorry to disturb you.' Stella seemed nervous, and rightly so. This was her hour before Church when she prepared herself to enter God's house. The staff knew she was not to be interrupted at this time.

'Yes?'

'It's Mrs Goldfire.'

'The photographs again, you mean?' She had already been in the old woman's room: there was no problem, she was quite safe.

'No, it's not that.' Stella seemed unable to look at her.

'Well?'

'You'd better come, Miss McBride. See for yourself.'

'Couldn't this wait until after Church? It would be more convenient.'

Stella was still refusing to meet her eye:

'Better to come now, I think.'

What could she have forgotten? Margaret's tear-stained tissue? That was only a scrap of paper. She hadn't touched anything else. She put aside her Bible and stood up:

'It had better be important.'

Stella in front, they climbed the stairs. What a blessing people had separate minds and only God could ever know the whole truth. It was His will that Mother had died without one word of love. In the sight of God that word would have been a lie. Knowing Margaret would have hurried to the bedside in a rush of daughterly weakness, He had commanded she was not to be contacted until it was too late. God was truth. He had guided and steadied her when she wavered.

Now, without Him, she was alone. His absence was a test. Surely now that she truly needed Him, He would come to her once more? Alone, she climbed the stair. Surely He would not abandon her? 'Whither thou goest I will go,' the words of Ruth were God's words also. He would be her guide and protector. They had reached the top corridor. Mrs Goldfire couldn't speak a word or point a finger of accusation at her.

The door stood open.

'In here, Miss McBride.'

The curtains had not been opened. The room was icy. The bed had been stripped, the furniture was bare. There was a sound like rain hammering against the window; cold rain. Exactly like Mother's room the day after the cremation service. A sudden gust of wind made the window-pane rattle.

So cold she was shivering. To steady herself she touched the end of the heavy mahogany bed. Its polished wood slid under her fingers, hard as ice. Was that Mother's perfume?

'Miss McBride? Sorry to have kept you waiting.' Stella was standing in the doorway. 'I was checking if the girls had finished in Mrs Goldfire's room.'

'Not in here, then? This isn't the room?'

'Of course not. Just for you to wait in for a moment. I didn't want any talk in front of the girls.' She paused. 'Are you all right, Miss McBride?'

Suddenly she felt weak. She wanted to sit down on the bed. She began trembling. 'It's cold in here.'

'Heating's switched off when the room's not used.' Stella went out into the corridor.

She remained where she was for several moments. She glanced

round the room; it was quite empty. Had Stella noticed any perfume? She daren't ask. She followed her out.

Sudden warmth. The sound of a hoover being used further down the corridor.

'We can go in now.'

Mrs Goldfire's room looked like all the rest: comfortable, lived in. A cold but sunny winter's day outside. No rain, not from this window.

'There's the photographs. I don't think they've been moved since I put them back that morning. But look here, at her hand.'

As always the old woman was in bed. Nothing had changed. She lay in the same position as last night and again this morning, her mouth slightly open, her breathing a steady sigh.

'See?' Stella was holding Mrs Goldfire's hand up for her to inspect. Scratch marks. 'Odd enough. But then look at this.' She turned the palm upwards.

There were several large bruises. Had she done that? Had she been gripping the old woman so tightly when she'd shown her Margaret's tears? When she'd waited for God's presence?

'Not that she seems to feel anything, poor soul.' Stella stroked Mrs Goldfire's arm.

It would only be a short walk to the church, but the streets looked wet. The rain had stopped: best if she took an umbrella in case, and the winter boots. Maybe even her heaviest coat.

Stella was still talking:

'She couldn't have done it to herself — she hasn't the strength. Miss McBride?'

Mrs Goldfire's hand was being held up for her to take and examine. Easily done. The bruising was severe and there were fingernail marks at the edges. 'You're sure she's in no pain?'

Stella shrugged. 'Who knows? She's pretty much away most of the time. But it's the whole business, really. The photographs, and now this. Someone must be doing it.'

Though the old lady's eyes were open she seemed quite unaware of what was happening around her. Her bedcap needed straightening.

'Have you any ideas, Stella?'

'None. She never gets any visitors, so it could only be one of the girls — which I can't believe — or one of the residents. Else there's only you, or me. And I know it's not me.'

Was she suggesting it might be her? She'd taken the old lady's hand and held it in hers. Nothing more. She had done nothing more.

'One of the residents? That's possible. Better keep an eye on them. It seems extraordinary, quite extraordinary. You're sure the photographs couldn't just have fallen over?' She was safe. No-one could know. No-one.

'Not really, Miss McBride.'

'A mystery, all right.' One last serious look, then a well-timed change of tone:

'And, Stella, the room next door: please see the heating's turned on and the bed made up. My nephew will be occupying it from now on.'

She went over to the window: a clear Edinburgh sky, scoured hard by the rain. Malcolm was playing in the garden, running silently up and down the path with his arms outstretched. A Stealth Bomber, presumably. Not intending to go to Church, it would seem. She would test his Commandments later. He wasn't wearing a coat — surely he'd be cold? Didn't Margaret know how to look after him? He needed a warm scarf: she'd have tied it herself and given his hair a playful ruffle before sending him out. Boys enjoyed being teased like that, though they pretended not to. The Stealth Bomber was grounded for the moment; tying his shoelaces. He could read to her again in the afternoon. Not a natural reader, unfortunately, but he had a lovely voice.

Really quite lovely.

It was time to get ready for Church. There she would find Him, and talk with Him, and pray for Him to be with her again.

Pray, and then beg.

14

That small model yacht your dad found somewhere is lying beached on the dressing-table. Tiny wee thing, like out of a cracker. You give it a quick sail round the palm of your hand. A bit tickly, especially when you make it go slower. Close your other hand over it and you will make night. Ease it up a little; dawn. Then morning, midday; late afternoon. Sunset lies across the edge of your palm, and again darkness. The mirror looks like a stretch of water lying on its side; you could try the yacht there. But be careful: you mustn't let your fingers touch the glass, or else you'll be back to that moment in the cottage when your mother screamed. Two yachts now. What's the mirror-yacht made of? Not metal, like the one you're holding, or it couldn't just appear out of nothing and then vanish when you take it away.

'We'll be leaving for the tour at two. In half an hour, mind.' Your mother's voice is coming from behind you. At the same time you can see her in the mirror, already miming the words perfectly.

You mime back at her:

'At two o'clock.' Can her reflection hear yours?

'Malcolm? I'm speaking to you.'

'Aye. Two o'clock. I'll be ready.'

'Don't be noisy, now. The old people are at their afternoon nap.'

You grab your jacket and, when you leave, are still clutching the toy yacht. Another quick exploration upstairs; with a bit of luck, Aunt Fiona-free.

The second floor. An old man with his back to you is limping his way to the end of the corridor. One of the residents, a bit livelier than Mrs Goldfire. He's wearing a dressing-gown, trousers and slippers, and has a stick in each hand. He jerks himself along, always seeming to be about to come to a halt, but at the last possible moment lurching into the next step. A wheeze, a gasp for breath, then forwards again. Two more steps and he'll have reached the wall at the end of the corridor. Where is he going? At least he's walking, sort of — more than your dad managed.

He's beginning to face round again. He's seen you.

'The legs went years ago.' He smiles while leaning the rest of himself into the turn. 'If I keep going, I won't stop. If I don't stop, I won't fall over.' His voice has more YES in it than NO. 'You'll be the nephew, then?'

'Aunt Fiona's my aunty.'

'That's the rumour, eh!' He shuffles himself towards you. 'Need to keep going, as I said. Chum me back to my room?'

You start walking beside him, very slowly.

A few wheezes further on:

'Good legs yourself, I see. Sorry to hear about your father.'

How could he have known your dad?

He stumbles suddenly:

'Don't stop, remember. My room is two to go. Number eight.'

A few more wheezes:

'Here we are. If you'll open the door for me, we'll go in as nice as ninepence. Thanks.'

Once inside, the old man staggers over to the fireplace, turns, then collapses back into his armchair. 'Home sweet home, eh!'

The room smells a bit, but not much. It's sunny outside, so you won't stay long. Above the mantelpiece there's a picture of an oil tanker with a red funnel and a white hull. The blue sea's lumpy with white waves; the sun is in the top right-hand corner.

'That was my ship. I worked on her, that is. Did the painting myself. Do you like ships?'

You're still holding your dad's yacht. Best not to let him see it, or you won't get away.

'I'm Jim Blackwood, by the way. And you?'

'Malcolm.' Now's the time to go.

Mr Blackwood picks up a tray from the stool beside him and clips it to his chair.

'My doings,' he explains. There's a newspaper, football coupons, tin of tobacco, tobacco papers, matches. 'I roll my own. Each one saves me ten pence. Be a rich man if I started chain-smoking.' He starts to make a cigarette. 'What's it you've got there?'

'A yacht, but not for sailing. It's a toy. I'd better be going.'

'Give's a wee look, son, eh?' The old man stretches out his hand and takes it. Strands of smoke-grey hair coil out from the top of his open shirt. He holds it up between his thumb and forefinger: 'This is a special kind of yacht: a bit of magic, and I think I can make it sail.'

Magic?

'I'd best be going. Really. My mum's waiting.'

'A very special boat, I'm telling you!' The old man nods seriously. 'Stand over here, Malcolm.' He grips your arm and pulls you to one side of his chair.

'Now, what do you make of this?'

He clears his 'doings' from the tray and places the model on it. 'Still water. The ship's becalmed. See?'

Big deal. You should pick it up and leave.

'But here's a bit of wind.' The old man blows softly.

Then all at once the yacht begins to move slowly forwards, by itself.

'Port,' he calls out. The small boat turns to the left. 'Starboard' — and it swerves to the right. All without being touched. 'Full steam ahead.' The model sails to the edge of the tray, then just in time he orders:

'Drop anchor.'

And it stops. Unbelievable.

'Magic, eh no?'

It must be. The boat's been sailing all by itself. Right in front of your eyes. Real magic.

'Fancy a go, Malcolm?'

'Me?'

'Just tell it to, and it'll start sailing where you want.' He smiles, places it in the centre of the tray, then nods at you to begin.

'To — the left.'

Nothing happens.

'You've got to say it in ship language, or it'll not understand what you want.'

You try again. 'Port.'

Still nothing happens.

'Louder, man. With a bit of ordering in your voice.'

'Port!' you call out more firmly.

The old man scratches himself on the chin and is about to reach over to light his cigarette — when he hesitates and, instead, lets his hand come to rest on the chair-arm.

That gesture of his is familiar: you've seen that kind of awkwardness, that wrong-handedness, somewhere before.

The ship still won't move.

Mr Blackwood shakes his head:

'You're not trying hard enough.' He shows you the underside of the model. 'See? There's no motor — nothing. You've got to keep thinking it where it's going. Do you understand?' He seems very excited. 'Just keep thinking it on, mind. I feel you're going to be lucky this time.'

The boat is placed in position.

'I'll give it a bit of a start. Then you carry on, eh?' He blows gently again and the boat begins gliding smoothly across the tray. 'All yours now.'

But already it's slowing down. You can see he's trying not to laugh. His left hand is raised in that awkward gesture again, this time to cover his mouth. Where have you seen someone do that before? So unusual, so familiar.

Your father's funeral, that's it! The minister. The minister fumbling clumsily at the open Bible with his left hand, to distract everyone while he reached down with his right to switch off the organ music tape. The old man's movement is like that: doing everything with one hand, the wrong hand. He's keeping his right hand under the tray. He needs it there for the 'magic', whatever that is.

Suddenly the model's started moving again. It's a cheat.

You reach down, grab the yacht and throw it on the ground.

'It's not magic. It's a cheat! And you're a bloody cheat as well!' You point your finger, stabbing it hard at him.

Then you lean close to his unshaven face and watery blue eyes that look for a second into yours before turning away. 'And you didn't know my dad either.'

You bend down to look for your yacht and pick it up.

'Just a wee joke, son. Nothing more.'

'No joke.' You stand in front of him with your fists clenched tight. 'It's no joke.'

He's stretching his hand out to you, showing a magnet he'd been holding under the tray:

'Here. I found it in my stuff just before we met in the corridor. And this too.' From the middle of his doings he picks up a small compass.

You'd like to throw both things to the ground. The cheat.

'Meaning no offence, son. Just to cheer you up. Would you like it?' He holds out the compass. 'As an apology of sorts. Go on.'

Like the minister switching off the music while pretending not to, as if the music was real and not a tape. Then talking about your dad as if he'd known him, when he hadn't. A cheat. Your mother had cried, but you'd not. You'd dug your fingers into the palm of your hand to stop yourself. You weren't going to cry for a cheat like that.

'Go on. A peace offering?'

You take a step back from him.

'It'll help your wee boat stay on course, and keep you right as well.'

The tiny needle is trembling as if it is alive. 'My dad gave me one.' A real lie.

The old man keeps looking at you.

'Yes. He gave me one with dials on it, and all that. So I would know things. So I'd know everything. Not just where I was going but the time and the date and where I was and what it meant.'

'What what meant? Here, son.' He puts it in your hand. 'Then you'll always have a spare.'

His watery eyes, his almost bald head. You'd like to shove him headfirst into the fireplace, and hear the *crack*.

You rush out of the room.

15

Mother is standing outside the sitting-room door.
No. No. She can't be.
Instead, there is:

- The Bible's hardness against her stomach.
- The gold embossed letters HOLY BIBLE that her fingers are tracing out.
- The hiss of the gas-fire warming her.
- The reading lamp beside her.

Mother can't be standing out in the hall because:

- She was burned to ashes years ago.
- She wouldn't wait but come in shouting, demanding, raging.

Further:

- The Sunday afternoon silence in the house.
- The residents are resting, asleep.
- Stella is out.
- Margaret and Malcolm are away on their bus tour.
- The stillness in her sitting-room.
- No-one is outside her door. No-one.

She has to remain motionless:

- Holding the Bible firmly on her lap.
- Holding its red-edged paper, its solid weight.

Or else:

- There will be a sudden knock at the door.
- Mother will come straight in shouting, demanding, raging.

She must:

- Grip onto the Bible's black leather binding.
- Press it so tightly to her she can hardly breathe.

So there will be no sudden knock at the door.

So Mother will not appear.

Not this afternoon, tomorrow afternoon, or ever.

Each afternoon must be exactly as planned and exactly the same. Exactly. By pressing God's Word close to her, everything will remain like this. God's Word is stronger than she is. Stronger than Mother.

Holding the Bible tight, trying to draw God's strength into herself so she will not:

- Get up from her chair.
- Climb the staircase to the top floor.
- Kneel at a stranger's bedside.
- Take a cushion in her hand to bring someone peace.

When she closes the curtains it will be evening, then night:

- The upstairs corridor in half-darkness.
- The line of closed doors.
- The sin of forgiveness.

Mother cannot be there. Nor her anger.

She has to:

- Put down the Bible, go to the door, open it and check.
- Put down the Bible, get to her feet, cross the room, go to the door, and check.

She has to.

And so:

Breathing heavily—

Her steps shaking—

Left and then right, and then left and then right...

Until she is leaning her forehead against the panelled frame.

Listening...

One turn will open the door.

Her back is towards the empty sitting-room — Mother might be behind her now. About to pull her round by the shoulders, about to start raging and screaming.

Clutching onto the smoothness of the door-handle.

She has to turn round to face her.

She's trying to turn round to face her.

Once.

Twice.

A third time. But she can't. She can't.

She can't. Her fingers can't let go the handle. Her neck and shoulders are too rigid to move.

At her back is the hiss of the gas-fire, the reading-lamp, her chair with the Bible on the side-table.

Waiting, listening:

To the quickness of her own breathing, to her fingernails scratching at the handle.

'Turn around.' Is *she* speaking aloud? Or Mother?

'Turn around.' Hardly even a whisper. The silence in the room almost touching her. Suddenly the door-handle's being turned. She clutches it. The door is being pushed open. She pushes back. She blocks it.

'Aunt Fiona?' Malcolm. It was Malcolm. Forcing her hand to be steady she opened the door:

'Keep your voice down. The old people are trying to sleep. You're not to shout, remember.'

'Sleep? But it's the middle of the afternoon.'

'Whatever time it is, you're not to shout.'

He was staring up into her face, in his hand he held something green. Green plastic.

'Mum said I was to show you this.' He made no move to offer it to her.

'When did you get back?'

'Just now. I was to come and show you this.' He remained standing a few feet away. Though it looked as if Margaret had done her best with a towel, his hair was still damp from the rain. There was mud on his shoes.

She would be friendly:

'Well, you'd better come in and show me.' A smile. Then, once she was seated, another smile.

Malcolm stretched his hand towards her. A small compass lay on his palm. His hand was sweating where he had held it tight.

She leant forward:

'It's a compass.'

'Yes.'

Not a very talkative child, but she would try to do her best. She picked it up. The plastic was uncomfortably warm, the underside sticky. A piece of green plastic with a clear top, no bigger than a wristwatch — with north, south, east and west marked in black, and a needle wobbling at the centre.

Made in China.

'Very nice.' She gave it back to him.

'It shows you things. Like where you are. Everything's got a direction.' Malcolm had taken the toy back and was looking closely at it while turning it from side to side. 'Shows you where you're going. All you have to do is look at the needle and it'll tell you.' He glanced up at her:

'You want a shot?'

She wanted to be left in peace. This was her rest time, her afternoon hour for sitting undisturbed with her Bible.

'Well—'

Abruptly Malcolm closed his fist around the compass and turned to go away. 'I knew you wouldn't. You'd be too busy, but Mum said I was to.'

'Now, Malcolm. I never said anything of the kind. I was about to observe — before you interrupted — that in the Bible, long before the compass had been invented, of course, God went in front of the Israelites wandering the desert "As a cloud by day and a pillar of fire by night".'

The damp smell from his hair. Warm and sweetish. He had Margaret's grey-brown eyes. Most of the sick-and-simple came eventually to have only one look in their eyes: a kind of pleading. None of them had thick black hair like this, but were bald or had their tufts of dryness brushed into pathetic curls.

'So, do you want a shot?'

'I'd like to very much. Thank you, Malcolm.'

Breathing in his warmth as she reached for the compass. An interested smile:

'Now then, what do I do?'

His warmth came a step nearer. She could smell the dampness in his hair much more now. She could breathe it in as he leant towards her.

'You decide where you want to go,' he was saying. 'Then hold the compass flat in your hand till the needle stops. Like this.' He positioned it in the centre of her palm. 'Where do you want to go?'

'Well, I — can't you make it work without my going somewhere?'

'No. Then it doesn't mean anything. It's where you're going to, from somewhere else, that matters. You need a direction. And you mustn't let it shake all the time.'

Malcolm was standing very close to her now. His hand steadying hers by pressing the compass more firmly onto her palm — if she hadn't pressed back, the compass would have fallen and probably broken.

'Will it be all right on my hand like this?'

'Fine — just don't shake.'

She watched as the needle gradually settled.

'So? Where do you want to go?'

She glanced up for a moment. There was her bookcase, opposite, with its dark-spined Commentaries and the set of Scott; the white marble mantelpiece; the gas-fire; the radiators under the bay-window; the door leading to the hall — her entire sitting-room as it lay beyond the circle of light made by the standard lamp. She didn't want to go anywhere. The half-darkness around her led only towards evening, towards the rooms upstairs. Her hand was trembling. Everytime he steadied the compass her palm was brushed by one of his fingers.

'So where do you want to go?'

'The fireplace.'

'All right,' he answered, without lifting his eyes from the compass. 'Now we turn it till the Magnetic North Line lies under the needle, and then we'll know exactly where the fireplace is.' He began rotating the small bubble of plastic.

If she reached out, she could cover his smaller hand with hers. She only wanted to help, of course. To join in. That was all. He was kneeling down to read the tiny printed marks on the compass. She couldn't see his face, only the tips of his ears, his heavy black hair and the back of his neck as he leant forward in concentration. Could she risk putting her hand on his shoulder: a gesture of friendliness, nothing more, like a grownup to a child?

Or would he pull away?

'North by north-west,' he said, straightening up from his crouched position.

She let her hand rest fully again on the chair.

He raised his head and looked straight at her:

'When you go to the fireplace from here, then it's north by north-west.'

'Thank you, Malcolm.'

'And now you'll know where everything else is too, mind. Not just the fireplace.'

He reached to pick up the compass from her hand and, without thinking, she closed her fingers over his. Meaning it as a joke, of course: the two of them holding hands.

Only for a few seconds.

His fingers were struggling to release themselves. She held them tighter, and pulled him towards her.

His face only inches from hers. The dampness in his hair, the glow on his skin.

'Let's see how strong you are, Malcolm. Try to get free? You can even use both hands if you want.'

But he stood as he was, stubbornly.

'Come on, Malcolm. It's a game. Let's see who's stronger.' She clenched her fist even tighter. 'Doesn't hurt, does it?'

'No.'

'Well, then. Come on.'

He looked down at her hand, then began trying to loosen her grip. Every time he'd prized one of his fingers free and moved onto the next, she recaptured the first one.

'It'll get broken.'

Could she pull him nearer? He was so worried about his stupid compass he'd never even notice. A steady tug, and his face was about to touch hers. Almost tasting the salt-sweetness coming from his skin. Nearer, and she could pretend to lick his ear, as a joke. Giving him his compass at the same time.

Suddenly he'd stopped struggling and taken a step back. But she'd not licked him. Had she? She gave a laugh to relax him. Then a smile:

'Giving up?'

He shrugged and looked away.

'Here.' She opened her hand. 'See? No harm done.'

She couldn't have licked him. She'd done nothing really. Couldn't he take a joke?

'Here.' She pushed the compass into his hand.

He didn't move. The stubborn boy wouldn't take it back. He wouldn't even look at her:

'You can have it if you want. I've got another my dad gave to me. I'd better go now.'

Then he turned and went out of the room without allowing her a chance to reply.

For several seconds she sits quite still.

She picks up the Bible.

She puts it down again. She can hardly breathe.

She stands up.

To visit Mrs Goldfire's room now: to kneel by the bedside to bury her face in the smell of blankets, to feel the touch of the old woman's hand on her head — could she risk going now, in the middle of the afternoon? To find a few moments' peace.

A few moments' rest...

16

Each part of the lawn is a different continent. At thirty thousand feet you can see a green patch of forest below, the separate houses of cities jumbled together like gravel, the ocean that's like dark earth because it's night as the Starfleet Raider passes above. Wings outstretched, the faintest hum from your engines: moving into Warp Factor 2. No-one can hear you or see you. Wall of meteorites ahead:

Evasive Action. Manual Control Override.

You veer left, your wing tip banked over until it's almost touching the ground. Then steadying again for a low-altitude skim across the States.

Your father's voice from Starfleet Command:

'Return to computed co-ordinates.'

Across the cities, the forests, the river that's hardened to a path of black pack-ice.

'Warp Factor 3.' Your father's voice is held at the same steadiness as his eyes when you went into his room.

Doesn't he know the back wall of the house will be straight ahead?

'Warp 4. Warp 5.'

He should tell you to turn to starboard.

'Force field ahead, ETA five seconds. Request change of course.'

Your head will crack like his did. Is that what he wants? His steady voice, his steady eyes. There's no-one else to help; you're accelerating over the-earth too high to be seen. No-one can shout to you or reach out to hold you. Only the voice of Starfleet Command:

'Warp 5. Warp 5.'

Crash landing into a small tree. Scanners into operation:

What is Aunt Fiona doing at the window? Her fingers are fiddling with the buttons of her blouse as if she was getting dressed. She's standing very still now. Not looking at you; staring straight out at nowhere. Not like five minutes ago when she was leaning close to you, with that brightness in her eyes.

She's rapped on the window. What's wrong?

She's rapping again. Angrily.

You've not done anything. You're standing in the garden, that's all.

She's shouting something but you can't hear because the window's closed. She's waving her arm. You should wave back.

Suddenly she's gone.

It'll be dark soon, and you'll be called in. Better keep Stealth Bombing until the last moment for then it'll just be stairs, corridors and rooms saying:

NO—NO—NO.

'Malcolm!'

Aunt Fiona's come out through the French windows onto the terrace. She shouldn't be shouting; you were told not to.

'It's rude to stare into windows.'

'I wasn't.'

She's started walking towards you:

'And it's rude to answer back.' Looking very angry; less than a yard away from you. Glaring at you. The middle button on her blouse isn't fastened. She couldn't have been getting dressed when you saw her; she's still wearing the same clothes as before. There's something white underneath.

'Do you understand me, Malcolm?'

'Yes.' Maybe you should tell her about the button? Show her you're trying to be helpful.

'Yes?' The same teacher pause.

'Yes, Aunt Fiona.'

'Have you learnt the Ten Commandments?'

'Nearly.'

'You will be tested later. Afternoon tea will be in ten minutes. You had better go in and wash.' She begins walking back to the house.

'Aunt Fiona, your blouse is undone.'

She stops, turns. Her face is bright red. She's striding back towards you, shouting:

'You little spy! How dare you! How dare you!'

You step backwards. She wants to hit you; not just with her voice this time. Another step.

'Just your button, I mean, Aunt Fiona. It's not—'

'Don't you dare answer back, you spy!'

'I'm not. Your button was—'

Her hands are grabbing at your shoulders, her fingers digging in hard, shaking you, her eyes *stab-stabbing*:

'What did you see? What did you see?'

'Nothing. It's just that your button—'

'I'm not talking about buttons.'

Marching you backwards now; your feet stumble against the edge of the path, then on to the grass.

'What did you see? I'm asking you.'

'Something white.' Hardly able to speak for the shaking she's giving you. 'White, where the button—'

'Never mind the button. Through the window, I mean, when you were spying on me.'

'Nothing. Nothing. I wasn't spying. I wasn't.' Why can't she believe you?

Then the marching stops.

She's leaning very close. 'You're sure?'

'Yes.'

Not even waiting for you to say, 'Yes, Aunt Fiona,' she stands up straight again. 'Well, this once I won't tell your mother. All right?'

'Yes.'

She's waiting for your correction — back to normal.

'Yes, Aunt Fiona.'

She smiles. 'I want you to be happy here, but that depends on you, Malcolm. If you persist in spying and in answering back, you will not be happy. I will see to that. But this once, nothing will be said.'

What's she on about? There's nothing to say anyway.

It's almost dark now. Over her shoulder you can see one or two lights have come on in the house, making the rest of the building look larger and gloomier. You can hardly make out her face any more.

Then, in a very different voice, she whispers:

'Malcolm?' She's speaking as if from far away: 'Malcolm, which button was undone?'

Is it another test? Like the Ten Commandments?

'Just one of them.'

She's looking at you very closely, half-smiling:

'Yes, Malcolm. But which one? Look and see.'

'It's been fastened up now.'

'Yes, but can't you remember which one it was? Maybe it's still a bit loose.'

Somewhere near the middle, just where she bulges. So you point:

'That one, I think.'

She smiles again. 'Just there, eh? Clever boy. I think you might be right, but it's getting so dark I can't see properly. Would you mind touching it for me, so as I'll know.'

But she *must* know. She must have refastened it herself after you told her, before she turned round all red-faced and mad.

'Go on, Malcolm. I'm not going to tell about your staring into windows, so you can do this for me.'

You touch one of the buttons in the middle.

'That's a good boy.' She leans closer to you, pressing the button against your fingers. 'Does it feel loose?'

'No.'

'Let's make sure.' Without her having taken a step she seems to be even closer. She's breathing quite loudly and, with one quick movement, she has undone the button. 'Was that how it looked?' She puts her hands back on your shoulders but not to shake you, just resting there.

'I can't see it any more.'

'Now, you fasten it up for me. Properly. Can't have your favourite aunt going around like something the cat dragged in.'

What does she want you to do that for? Can't she fasten her own buttons? Her hands are trembling — maybe she's getting cold. If she stood still, you could do it quicker, but she's started shivering, making it much harder for you. She must be really cold. She'll be angry if you don't hurry up. The white material's so slidy underneath, the button-hole and the button keep slipping apart. Also, she keeps pressing nearer; as if trying to help, but really making it harder.

You've finished, at last.

'Clever boy. Did you like doing that for me?'

Like it? You like that she's not being snappy and angry any more. 'Yes, I—'

'Good boy. That's our secret then. And I won't tell on you for staring into windows and then answering back. Agreed?'

Whatever she's talking about, she wants you to say Yes, so you do.

An abrupt change in her voice, back to normal:

'It's got quite cold now. Time we went in.' She begins to walk towards the house. 'Come along, Malcolm. Afternoon tea in ten minutes. You'll need to wash your hands. You can go in by the kitchen.' She walks off towards the French windows.

At the back door you halt for a moment: the metal handle makes you shiver when you touch it. Not like the soft material of her blouse, not like her warmth.

17

Spying on her; pretending her button was undone. The excuse being, no doubt, that he was at a difficult age. Now there was an evening with Margaret to be got through. At least she could have these few minutes to herself while Malcolm was being put to bed in his new room. She would rally: a quick chat, then they could work on the jigsaw together. An intense conversation was the last thing her sister needed at the moment, so she would be tactful but firm. She was so, so tired all of a sudden. So weighted down that any conversation, let alone one about Mother, was going to be quite beyond her.

Her sitting-room felt cosy: curtains closed, gas-fire hissing away. To go to bed and sleep, sleep, sleep — that was all she wanted. No visits, no pills — nothing but letting her eyes close for a long, long time...

Had she dozed off? Her sister was sitting opposite now. Right, begin:

'Before we start, Margaret, I want you to know that any talk we have about Mother is going to upset me.' She held up her hand to stop her sister's inevitable interruption. 'Now, I'm not wanting to make you feel guilty, just wanting to set things straight from the beginning.' She carefully looped in the black ribbon and closed the Bible. 'I should have thought you must be having a difficult enough time as it is, at the moment.'

'Fiona, I—'

'So let's not add to it.' A good clear start. A smile to give her sister confidence. Keep things short and to the point, and they might even get the jigsaw finished by bedtime. 'Now, what was it you wanted to say?'

'Fiona, you've not really understood. I don't want to talk about our mother but—'

'I can understand how hard it is, of course. You don't really want to, but I'll help all I can.' Another smile. A glance over at the jigsaw and the scatter of pieces to be fitted into position. One was completely green — it had to be either from the tree next to the railings or from the small lawn in front. There was no other green in the picture. Unless the ivy? — but that was the wrong shade.

'Fiona?'

It had to be the ivy. The shade was deceptive in a single piece like that, but she wasn't so easily misled. Only one small trail of ivy, so the rest had to belong on the borders of sandy brickwork. A whole pile of them was already sorted out. She snapped the piece into place. Success.

An encouraging look:

'You talk, and I'll listen.'

'I never mentioned our mother.'

'Now's your chance.' Her sister really needed help to get started: 'About the way she treated Father, maybe? Always chipping away at him. It was *her* house. *Her* family he was marrying into — never the other way round?' A questioning look this time. A polite pause to let Margaret respond. No such luck, and so another try:

'She never let up, did she? The more he tried to be as she wanted, the more she looked down on him. She'd have him nearly in tears. He never cried, of course. You and I did sometimes. But not Father.'

'But, Fiona, you know he did. Not just once either. She tried to destroy him.'

What a bitter voice. So much for her sister's first contribution: wanting to start an argument. She was having to do all the work herself to get Margaret talking. Her little sister was in too anxious a state for that kind of discussion. Understandably distressed. Quite the wrong time and quite the wrong topic, though Margaret herself had chosen it. She was in a highly emotional state and needed to be comforted, also to be reminded of the facts. The record to be set straight and that would be that.

Father crying?

Straight forward projection on Margaret's part, of course, a natural defence mechanism at a time of grieving. Fiona put an obvious brickwork piece into its pile — it would slot in perfectly against the green — and looked over to her. A slight pause to emphasize the seriousness of what she was about to say, then speaking steadily, calmly, she explained for the second time:

'You cried sometimes, and so did I — but not Father.'

Another pause to let her sister reflect upon the truth of this. How sad she looked, her eyes especially. Their glance was so desolate and inward-looking: a woman who desperately needed comfort. Time for a quick, encouraging smile but one that also acknowledged the unhappiness her little sister must be feeling. Maybe even take her hand?

They sat without speaking for several seconds, then there was the touch of Margaret's hand on her own, reaching out for support. Quite unexpected. A good sign.

So, another smile, even more encouraging:

'Don't worry, Margaret, even the worst times pass. They do, you know.' A sensitive squeeze in response, then, indicating her empty cup:

'More tea?'

'What are you talking about, Fiona?'

'About Mother, of course. That's what you wanted.' Best to keep moving things along; the faster forward the sooner finished:

'It must be particularly hard for you, coming back to live in this house, just now of all times. You're distressed. Quite understandable. We must try better ways of taking your mind off things. Pity the weather's been so bad, Malcolm would have loved the Zoo. I'll pray to God for a clear, sunny day!' Her sister needed cheering up, that was all. Tomorrow they would go somewhere together. If fine, the Zoo. If not, the cinema. Another smile. She should suggest the two of them work on the jigsaw now; something might still be made of the evening.

'Well then, Fiona, if you insist on it. There is something I've wanted to talk about concerning our mother, but haven't until now. Her funeral. You didn't cry at her funeral.'

Sunday was supposed to be a day of rest. Nearly nine-thirty. How long was this going to go on? She felt very tired all of a sudden. One last effort, and that ivy covering the brickwork and side wall would almost be finished. Something in the day achieved, at least.

Margaret kept on:

'I cried. I couldn't help it, even after all that had happened. But you didn't — and when we got back home you accused me of betrayal.' A pause to get her voice under control. 'Of betrayal, hypocrisy and goodness knows what else, Fiona. You screamed and raged at me.'

'I don't remember.'

'I do.' Margaret was looking straight at her. 'Also the fact that you didn't let me know about the funeral until the very last minute. Why not?'

Outside a car's tyres swished along the wet street. It must have started raining again. Fiona shivered. The longer this went on, the more upset her sister would become. She should be firmer. Still friendly, of course, but firm. For her sister's own good:

'As I explained then, I couldn't get hold of you. And anyway, you were expecting Malcolm at the time, so I didn't want to cause you any further problems—'

'Being pregnant was not a problem, Fiona.'

'Really, Margaret, this is ancient history — and best left at that.' Was her sister wanting some kind of apology? Not really merited but, in the interests of keeping the peace and helping her, she would do her best. There'd still be time for the jigsaw, but only just — maybe just the ivy, and make a good start on the wall. 'I'm sorry. It wasn't easy for me, you know. It meant I was left to see to all of the arrangements myself. If I was so insensitive to say those things, then I apologise. I didn't mean them. I was probably upset and took it out on you, on my little sister.'

'You certainly did.'

'Well, I'm apologising now.'

'Thank you. But that's not what's important.'

'No?' For God's sake, what did the woman want? 'Well, what is?'

'It might be "ancient history", as you call it, but it's still our lives.'

What was that supposed to mean? A glance over at the clock: it was getting late.

'Our lives, Fiona. Do you understand?'

'No.'

'*Did* you understand, then?'

'When?' Her sister seemed to be wandering far from the point.

'The day I left home after her screaming at me for the hundredth time, and me screaming back about what a crazy bitch she was. Remember? You carried my bags. You helped me find a taxi and then a room.'

The conversation was really getting out of hand. Perhaps she should just press on with the jigsaw by herself. She picked up one of the green pieces — bound to be ivy.

'Well? What was wrong with that?'

'Nothing. I was very grateful. But you never once said anything about why I was going. We sat in the taxi and you told me funny stories about what it would be like living in a bedsitter.'

'You needed cheering up.'

'Yes, yes. I know I did. But you never once mentioned our mother, never once told me I was doing the right thing. And afterwards you came straight back here and carried on as if nothing had happened.'

'I lived here. What else was I to do?'

'Jesus Christ, Fiona, I don't know. Tell me I wasn't making it all up.'

'Making what up?'

'Our mother — and the way she treated us.'

'She was a bit difficult at times, granted. But—'

'Difficult? Oh, Fiona.' Then the tears started.

Her sister was clearly more distressed than she'd realized. Distressed and angry. But next of kin were often like that, displaced anger. Much better to let her get it off her chest, then they could return to normal life. The jigsaw would have to wait — a pity — but Margaret was more important.

Luckily enough, the tissues were still on top of the TV. She brought them over, placing them on her sister's lap. Margaret should have a good cry and get this over with once and for all.

Her sister was staring at her, red-eyed, with tears streaming down her face.

'I don't want any bloody tissues. I didn't want to talk about our bloody mother anyway,' she shouted. Then she picked up the box and threw it to the floor.

'Margaret!' What kind of behaviour was that? And the language, too. 'Margaret, try not to—'

'No bloody lectures either.'

There was a silence. Her sister continued sobbing. Another car passed outside.

What did she want? A kiss and a cuddle, and someone to tell her everything was all right? They weren't children any longer. She was about to sit down again when Margaret took her hand.

For several seconds neither of them spoke. She stood motionless. What was she expected to do now?

The clock chimed quarter to ten.

She stood closer and put her free arm round her sister. What should she say? 'There, there' sounded like she was talking to a small child who'd hurt herself. How did that old nursery rhyme go:

'You've hurt yer finger, pair wee man; yer pinkie, dearie me.' Once started, she couldn't stop it going round and round in her head. 'You've hurt yer finger—'

This was her sister who had just lost her husband.

'Yer pinkie, dearie me.' She bit her lip to try stopping the rhyme, then began stroking Margaret's hair. Finally she eased herself free of Margaret's grip, bent down to retrieve the box of tissues and handed her one of them. She sat down.

'Feeling better?' she asked a moment later.

'Yes.' Her sister half-smiled at her:

'Sorry about that.'

'Never mind. All over now.' Fiona smiled back. There'd be a few more tears and apologies, another cup of tea perhaps, then they'd go off to bed. Two tablets and a long dreamless sleep. Maybe she should offer Margaret one?

'Don't worry. You're distressed at the moment — perfectly understandable. We'll say nothing more about it. Now then, Margaret, shall I make us some more tea?'

'Tea? You wanted us to talk about our mother.'

That had been her sister's idea, but she would let it pass.

'Look, that's all ancient history, as we said.' A reassuring pat on the arm. 'A cup of tea, a good night's sleep and in the morning—'

'Why don't you listen, Fiona? Our mother—'

'Mother wasn't crazy. A bit difficult now and again. Some mothers are. You wanted to leave, so you left. It's not a question of right or wrong. Or of anybody being crazy: her, or you. Or even me for that matter!' That should lighten the tone a bit. 'It's just life: children grow up and leave home everyday.'

'So why didn't you?'

This was turning into an interrogation. Distress excused only so much. She would be sensitive to Margaret's feelings, of course, but truthful:

'Our parents needed looking after. Once they got older, especially. Once they couldn't look after themselves.' A pause for emphasis. 'It was my duty.' She didn't want to make her sister feel guilty, but facts were facts.

'What does that make me then, Fiona? A bad girl? Is that how you see me?'

Enough. She'd been sympathetic, she'd been understanding. But enough was enough. Margaret needed to calm down, have a good night's sleep, and things would look better in the morning. She stood up.

'I think it's time we went to bed. I can give you something to help you sleep.'

'I don't want—'

'You don't want a pill. Fine. You don't want to sleep. Fine. You can sit here and tear Mother to shreds all night if you want to. I'm going to bed.'

Margaret was getting to her feet:

'Fiona, please, there's no need to—'

Was her sister really trying to stop her leaving?

'Goodnight, Margaret.' Firmly but politely. Then out the door, closing it behind her, crossing the hall, hurrying up the stairs — away.

Away from her sister and her anger. Her sister who never once helped care for Mother, who never once wrote or phoned to ask how she was, but turned up immediately she needed help herself. Her sister who lost her temper the moment things weren't exactly the way she wanted. They could have chatted together, they could have finished the jigsaw. Margaret could have asked about her for a change, about how she'd coped with Mother, about how she coped now. She'd done everything, and single handed, too. No professional staff in those days: up and down the stairs at all hours, bringing Mother hot drinks, changing the bed. Nothing had been too much trouble. In the final weeks she'd hardly slept.

The top floor, at last, along the corridor and into Mrs Goldfire's room. Onto her knees by the bed and burying her face in the scent of the old woman's blankets. Breathing in the sweetness as deeply as she could. Holding the old lady's hand. How could her sister behave like that: trying to make her unhappy just because *she* was? If she couldn't conduct herself properly she would be asked to leave, there was nothing else for it. The old lady's hand felt so fragile. It was dry and almost without flesh. A clutch of twigs bound together at the wrist. Her sister's shouting, her throwing things around and her endless interrogation, that was all over and finished with. Soon the old lady's hand would begin stroking her hair, and she would feel comforted. Soon she would feel loved.

Mrs Goldfire had begun to snore feebly. Whenever she squeezed the old lady's hand there was a faint sigh. Was she hurting her? She hadn't meant to scratch her last night. She'd better be more careful.

'I'm sorry, Mother. I'm sorry. Forgive me.' Already she could feel the beginnings of the peace that was going to come. If she really tried to say everything that was in her heart, surely she would be accepted once more. Accepted, and forgiven.

And loved.

Smoothing the old woman's hand in her own, she began:

'Mother, please. To forgive, if only we—'

What was she saying? And what was she nearly crying for? She swallowed and held the old woman's hand against her face.

'To forgive—'

She bit into the blanket to stop herself. Her teeth were clenched until she was almost choking on the words that kept forcing themselves out.

The centre light had clicked on.

Margaret was looking down at her: 'Fiona? I heard someone cry out.'

She made no reply.

'What's happening? Are you all right?'

She pulled herself up to her feet. 'What do you mean: am I all right? Of course I am. It was Mrs Goldfire. I heard her crying, so I came in. She's settled now. We should leave her.'

'Fiona? What is it? What were you doing?'

'Looking after one of my residents, of course. She was quite out of it, poor thing. I'm going to bed now. Let me pass.'

'Oh, Fiona.' Her sister was coming towards her, her arms open.

'Let me pass, will you?' She would knock Margaret out of the way if she had to. 'Let me *pass*.' She needed to be in her own room. Two pills, three — and she'd be asleep in seconds. 'Please.'

Into the corridor. No rooms mattered now, no doors. Down the stairs, and keep going. Her sister was behind her, calling after her. Turn, and deal with her:

'People are trying to sleep, Margaret. Go to bed. Goodnight.'

'But, Fiona—'

'Goodnight.' And keep going.

Almost there. All the lights blazing behind her.

Her door. Her room. Her pills. Quickly. By the bed.

'Fiona, what's wrong? What were you doing up there? What's going on?'

Two pills by her lamp. A new packet in the drawer. But her sister first.

'This is my bedroom. I'm going to bed, Margaret. I'm tired. It's been a long day, and Mrs Goldfire was the last straw.'

'You were kneeling by her bed.'

'She'd been crying. She was upset and needed looking after. That's my job — are you trying to tell me my job now?' A new packet. She'd be ripping the cellophane off with her teeth in a minute.

'Let me help.'

'I can open it perfectly well, thank you. There.' Twenty-four pills, each in its own plastic window. Pop the extra one. Three pills; asleep in three minutes.

'But you called out "Mother".'

Swallow one. Swallow two. Swallow three. In a few moments, sleep.

'That was Mrs Goldfire. As I said, she was upset.'

Already she felt easier. Margaret stood with her arms hanging loosely by her sides and looking so needy, so abandoned. Poor little sister without a husband any more; what she really wanted was someone to care for, someone to need her. Well, she'd got a son, hadn't she?

'It was your voice, Fiona.'

'Don't you worry yourself, Margaret. I know how to look after my residents, I've been doing it long enough. When Mrs Goldfire's really poorly I pretend to be her daughter. Harmless deception. She goes to sleep and forgets.' A smile and a yawn; a broad enough hint, surely. 'Good plan for us as well, don't you think?'

She gave another yawn, a real one this time. She was tired now. Head on the pillow and she'd be away from all this in a few seconds.

'I'm going to bed, Margaret.'

She picked up her dressing-gown and went into her bathroom, called out a firm goodnight and closed the door.

Staring down at the crisscross tiles: following the nearest line from the side of the bath to the radiator at her left foot. Her little sister could never have done this job: one husband to look after, and the poor thing went to pieces. Fiona had nursed both their parents, then dozens of the sick-and-simple. Scores of them, in fact. Now she was having to look after Margaret. And Malcolm, too; making friends with him, making him feel at home, trying to cheer him up despite his noise and his nosiness. Retracing the next line from the radiator back to the edge of the bath. She stood up. A wash now, and bed.

Back to her bedroom.

Margaret had gone, and taken her complaints with her. Thank goodness. Sleep, at last.

Was someone sitting on the edge of her bed?

Her eyes were so heavy. Trying to keep them open, to force the lids up. But they kept sliding down, closing. Was someone there? Becoming harder each time to raise them by will-power. The light was switched off; had she done it herself? She was so tired. She must have done. Or was she dreaming? Not enough strength to speak or even raise her hand.

Was someone there? Margaret?

But why didn't she say something?

A hand was being placed gently upon her head, stroking her hair. Tears had started to prick behind her eyelids. She was going to cry. Someone was touching the side of her face, smoothing her hair. 'Stop, stop!' she wanted to say, but couldn't speak out loud. 'Stop!' She swallowed, trying to hold the tears back. One ran slowly down her cheek and was brushed away. Then another. There was no reason to cry, no reason at all.

18

You had been asleep until—

'What were you doing?' Your mother is outside in the corridor.

'Let me pass, will you?' Aunt Fiona has shouted back.

The drowning had started immediately you'd got into your new room. You'd tried everything, even looking at the bits of invisible writing you'd done with Sonny — blank and useless. Stupid passwords for stupid kids. Then you'd played with the model yacht, sailing it on the bedside table, pretending that's what your dad would have done — but you knew that's all it was, just playing. And all the time the drowning was rising more and more around you, seeping into you, until you felt dead like he was.

Getting wakened now was like coming back from being dead, so now you'll have to begin all over again. Sitting up like your dad. Holding your breath. Staring into the darkness without moving a muscle.

You are back in the garden with Aunt Fiona—

Keep staring straight ahead to stop the drowning.

She's walking slowly towards you, undoing the first button, the second—

Clench your fists or the drowning will come. The dirty black water will begin rising.

The third button. Her finger stroking the edge of the material, pressing nearer you—

You had been tip-toeing over some thin ice on Robson's field with Sonny: each step making silver-white lines zig-zag faster than your eyes could follow.

The noise of the two women's voices, going down to the next floor, turns the stairs and corridors into so many cracks running through the darkness of the house.

But when the ice didn't hold...

A door slams downstairs.

...the clouds and sky lying scattered at your feet: they had become pieces of your aunt's unfinished jigsaw.

The door slams again: the cracks are cutting into your room.

Stare hard, stare to keep the cracks from coming nearer.

Your body so rigid now that no-one could make you slip and then fall to one side like he did.

The silence is so cracked across, the drowning comes rushing nearer...

'Port.' Your father's voice from somewhere near, guiding you. You are to get out of bed. You will have to make yourself even harder. You mustn't move. Be ready to scream. To tell him to go away.

'Port.'

Relax even slightly, and the darkness will rush to choke you; you will fall to one side, towards that *crack*.

'Port.'

His voice is inside you, it is much stronger than you. Every muscle and bone is clenched as rigid as you can, but his voice relaxes them and makes them move as he wants. Already you are climbing out of bed. Struggling not to, but you can feel the carpet under your bare feet.

You are standing up.

'Starboard.'

Your body turning to the right, your right foot takes a step forwards. Then your left.

'Full steam ahead.'

Towards the door. One step, then two, three. Not even needing your arm raised to steady yourself, your father's voice supporting you instead. The handle. Turn and—

'Port.'

Looking down the long corridor. The small side-lamp marking the top of the stairs and, beyond it, the darkness at the other end. The draught at the back of your neck is your father's breath blowing you carefully forwards.

'Ahead. Steady as she goes.'

One step, a second, third. The downstairs clock's slow tick charts the silence around you as currents and hidden shallows.

A door is standing wide open and the light is full on. Again you are going to see the old woman Aunt Fiona forced you to look at: her shrunken mouth, her tears as she slid heavily to one side. You don't want to, but even before you hear his voice speak you know what is going to happen next.

'Port.'

And you turn into the room. The crumple of bedclothes and old age: Mrs Goldfire is exactly the same as before.

'Steady as she goes.'

To the side of the bed.

'Drop anchor.'

Your father's strength reaching out your hand. Touching the coldness, the smoothness, the hardness of glass.

His strength closing your fist, clasping, then raising your arm. Holding the small ornament up for you to see. There's your reflection looking out at you.

'Starboard. Starboard.'

You turn, switch off the light, leave the door closed behind you as it should be.

Sitting up in bed again with the snow ornament in your hands. You shake it and watch the flakes swirl round the solitary piper. They go slower and slower, settling on his shoulders, his pipes, and drift into a heap at his feet. Now you can see his reddish face and his brown beard painted on to the front of his uniform. He has blue dots for eyes. You shake him up again and the snowstorm starts. He must be happier when it's snowing, the flakes dancing round to his music. When it's still, he looks very lonely playing his pipes and nothing happening.

Another quick snowstorm.

Then again before it settles. You can't stop, you don't want him to feel alone in there, trapped.

Shaking it, shaking it.

Your father's calming voice:

'Steady. Steady as she goes.'

So, the piper and his snowstorm cupped in your hands. Held there, safe. You'll look after him. He won't be lonely: he won't need to play and play until he runs out of breath.

You should place him under your pillow: a bit of a lump, but there's still plenty of room for your head.

Reaching into the darkness for the the softness of the pillow, and beneath it, the firmness.

This is how it will feel when Aunt Fiona takes your hand to touch the white lace where she bulges, how she'll pull your face into the warmth.

Your hand grasping at the lump under the pillow. This is how it will feel: warm, soft and firm at the same time. Safe.

You say the words, aloud:

'Warm. Safe.'

She will unbutton her blouse and place your hand there. Warm and safe. No drowning can happen.

Not until the house hardens into ice around you; not until the darkness cracks under your feet.

19

She clenched the white coldness of the sheet and lay still.

Then clenched it tighter.

Two-four-five on the digital alarm. Night-silence, and rain. Darkness.

Half-coming out of a dream to find someone already entering her. Clenching the cold sheet she listened hard to the rain hitting against the stonework, against the glass pane, then soaking with a steady drip-drip into the lilac bush at the back wall while the wind rose and fell. Someone's unspoken presence lay between the separate drops: the taste and smell of their skin, their hair.

The top corridor, the closed doors, the spy-holes. The sick-and-simple at rest, apart from Malcolm's room, where she'd smelt Mother's perfume. She walked to the end of the corridor and at once walked back again. Like a guard on duty. She turned again, and again marched the length of the corridor. She wouldn't stop to open any of the spy-holes and glance inside — not tonight. Tonight she would keep marching, and keep guarding. *Left-right left-right*; up and down the central strip of carpet past Mr Davidson's room, Mrs Connaught, Mr Byrd, Mr Wells, Mrs Goldfire. They were in her care. Anything might happen. She was their only protector. *Left-right, left-right*. She had so much energy — if she wanted she could march even faster. She wasn't tired. Not one bit. Margaret would be asleep downstairs, resting from a day's doing nothing. Not like her. *Work, work, work. March, march, march. Left-right, left-right.*

Malcolm was in the empty room now. He needed her protection. They had come to her: refugees with a few suitcases, a couple of plastic bags and a small rucksack. She'd taken them in: her widowed little sister, her young nephew. It was her Christian duty, and she cared for them. She should glance in and check he was settled in his new room. That was all she would be doing. Checking he was settled, nothing more. She looked down the length of the empty corridor. All she wanted was to see if he was sleeping peacefully. She slid the spy-hole cover to one side.

She could see nothing. There was no night-light burning. She waited for a moment, staring into the darkness as hard as she could, but only the faintest outline of the furniture was visible. She could see nothing of Malcolm. It would be better if she went in. Only for a moment, of course. Just to check. She'd be very quick.

Pulling the handle towards her to ease the catch, she turned it as soundlessly as she could, opened the door and stepped in. She closed it behind her in case the corridor light woke him. He was breathing regularly. By the faint light coming over the top of the curtain she could just make out his head on the pillow. She tiptoed across the room to open the curtains a fraction.

She could see him better now. He looked so peaceful. Secure. Never once had she known such tenderness from Mother as Malcolm received every single day from Margaret. What had he done to deserve it? He lay there, breathing easily; his head half on the pillow, half slipping to one side, one arm trailing out over the quilt. Margaret could smooth his hair if she wanted, take his hand and put it back under the warm blankets. Margaret could hold him and kiss him goodnight. Margaret could love him.

He'd only moved in to the room a few hours ago and already the floor was a battlefield of aeroplanes, spaceships, police-cars, soldiers and spacemen. How could anyone read so many comics at the same time? On the bedside cabinet was that miniature yacht that had belonged to his father, and some scraps of paper. What could he find to write about? She held one of the pieces up to the light. Blank, but very crackly and dry. The room was a bad enough mess already, without litter everywhere; she pocketed them. She'd speak to him about the aeroplanes and spacemen tomorrow. Now that the curtains were open she could see the yacht lay in the middle of scratch marks freshly scored across the polished wood. Her good furniture. She pocketed the yacht as well.

A moment later she was sitting on the edge of the bed with Malcolm's hand in hers. Everything was going to be all right: she needed a few minutes like this just to show she wasn't angry with him. That was all. A few minutes' peace — was that too much to ask for? Anyone else would have woken him and given him a good row for having ruined the bedside cabinet like that. Not to mention the noise he'd been making all day, the answering back, spying in windows and the rest. But she wasn't like that: she understood the distress, the unhappiness he must be feeling.

The sense of loss.

Poor boy. She pressed the back of his hand very lightly, then began stroking it, and could not help herself raising it to feel its touch upon her cheek. Half bending forward to hold it there she gazed down at him. He was deeply asleep. With his fingers she brushed the side of her face, her eyelids, then down to her mouth. She should put his hand carefully back on the covers, get up and leave. She should go now, but already she had begun drawing his fingers along her lips. Such delicacy. Softness.

Looking down at him in the half-light she could make out his eyes and the outline of his nose. She could almost feel the smoothness of his cheek. Her lips parted, letting his fingers press against her tongue. She must, must stop. She wanted to lick each finger. Taking the first one slowly into her mouth. But she mustn't. What if Malcolm woke? She was already licking the second. Then the third. What if she were found here? She should give the back of his hand one last kiss, then let go. She had to.

She bit hard.

Your hand hurts. The light's on. Aunt Fiona's sitting on the edge of your bed.

'It's all right, Malcolm,' she stroked his hand. 'I'm here.'

'What is it? What—?' You should try to sit up, to pull your hand free.

'You must have been having a bad dream. I was next door, seeing to one of the residents, and came through. It's all right now.' She made to put her arms round him, but he drew away.

Her eyes are staring down into yours. So greedily. You press back into the pillow.

'Where's Mum?'

'She's in her room, sleeping. It's late. You were calling out, so I came. Just a bad dream — there's nothing to worry about now. Go back to sleep.' A goodnight smile, then lifting her hand casually, as if to ruffle his hair.

Pressing yourself deeper into the pillow, your back deeper into the bed.

'I'm not going to hit you.' A light-hearted laugh.

You weren't expecting her to. But something else? The greed in her eyes; her fingers grabbing at you.

'Why are you here, and not Mum?'

'Your mum's in her bed.' She sat back a little. All she'd wanted was to reassure him, just to stroke his hair as Margaret would have done.

'Come on, Malcolm. Close your eyes. Everything's all right. Would you like me to stay until you're asleep again?'

'My hand's sore.'

'You must have slept on it. Sometimes I wake up and my arm's all pins and needles because of the way I've been sleeping. Would you like me to rub it better? That always works.' She should stop talking. She should get up and leave; let him go back to sleep and forget everything. There would be the touch of his hand on her lips to remember and the sleepy friendliness in his voice. Would that be enough? Could she risk ruffling his hair now? If he pulled away, what would be left for her?

She's not stood up yet. She's not wearing a blouse any more but a nightdress with buttons down the front, and a dressing gown. She's pressing the buttons and her warmth towards you as she leans nearer. None of them are unbuttoned.

'It's really sore.'

Maybe she really had hurt him. Better to check.

'Poor boy, poor boy.' She took his hand. 'Where is it sore?'

'My fingers.'

'Let me see.' She lifted them to the light. The marks where she had bitten were clear. She stroked them gently. 'Is that better?'

'Mmm. A little.'

He was letting her take his hand, letting her rub its warm skin smoothness. 'That feel good, Malcolm?'

'Really sore. Not just pins and needles.'

Why doesn't she undo her blouse? Should you pretend one of her buttons is undone again and do it up for her?

'I know. Poor boy.' The marks would fade by tomorrow morning. Surely. 'You're a brave soldier though, not to cry.' His hand lay warm in hers.

She might go at any moment — then the drowning would start all over again. Already the silence is hardening around you, except where she's holding your hand.

'A brave soldier. Some boys run to their mothers for the littlest things, but you don't. You're brave.'

'Mum would kiss it better.'

Her mouth had gone dry. 'Would she?'

'Yes.'

She's leaning so close to you, you can see the buttons strain very slightly. You should let your hand slide over them once she's finished kissing your fingers.

When he didn't pull away she kissed the bite-marks one by one. He wanted her to do it, he had *asked* her to do it: she was comforting him, not doing anything wrong.

'That better?' she asked after each kiss.

It would be enough that she'd kissed his fingers — she would remember the taste of his skin, and his complete trust. They had done nothing wrong. 'My brave soldier,' she whispered at the end.

'But you said you'd stay until I was asleep again. You said you would.'

If he needed her just to be there, then it was all right. He needed someone. If his own mother couldn't look after him when he had nightmares — Margaret was exhausted with grief, poor woman — then she would stay and do her best. She would be careful: she'd sit with him for a short time, nothing more.

If you pretend to fall asleep, you can start to move your hand nearer to her.

His eyes were closed, but he was breathing too quickly to be asleep.

The very faintest whisper:

'Malcolm?'

She reached forward to smooth his hair, letting her fingers gently stroke the side of his face:

'Malcolm?' Still too softly to be heard.

It would be reassuring to give him a favourite aunt's goodnight kiss upon his brow. That same rapid breathing. He must still be awake and must know she was there.

The model yacht she'd picked up earlier, she should have it ready in her hand in case she felt him withdraw.

She leant closer. She was his favourite aunt giving him a comforting goodnight kiss after his nightmare, that was all.

His brow first. He was certainly awake, and he had let her kiss him.

Then leaning even closer until her lips were almost touching his.

No. She must stop.

'I'd nearly gone off with this.' Quickly she showed him the yacht:

'You're a naughty boy, it marked the table. Look.' She pointed out the scratches. Taking his hand to make his fingers trace the cuts in the wood. 'See how deep it is. That was your small boat. Now, I don't want to give you a row—'

'I'm sorry.'

'—especially as you've just been given a room of your own.

'I'm sorry.'

Still holding his hand. 'Your mother would be very angry if she knew. She wouldn't be as forgiving as I am.' She smiled and patted his cheek, letting her hand remain against it. 'So, if we can be friends — nothing will be said.' Stroking his cheek gently; giving his hand the slightest pressure, her finger tracing a line on the softness of his skin up to his wrist, then from side to side just under the cuff of his pyjamas.

No. Stop. Stand up. Say goodnight and leave. Stand up, say goodnight and leave.

'We can be friends, can't we?' Moving closer to his mouth again.

Her voice almost a whisper once more. Secretive; boys liked secrets. 'Friends don't tell on each other. I'll not tell your mother about what you've done.'

The side of his face and the lightness of the hair at his ear — almost absently, her hand was gently brushing to and fro. Speaking so softly. Her mouth nearly dry. A little closer:

'If we're friends I won't say anything. It will be our secret.'

'Cross your heart and hope to die?'

'Of course, Malcolm.' A smile:

'Is *that* where your heart is? I can't feel it beating.'

Leave. Leave. Stand up say goodnight and leave.

She has put her hand on your chest. She's sliding it inside your pyjama jacket. So warm and cool at the same time.

'That's better. I can feel it now. A good strong heart.'

Her hand doesn't keep still but has started passing backwards and forwards over your skin.

'That's yours crossed, now—'

She's looking straight at you, but far away, and talking as if to herself:

'Now, you're to cross mine like that.' Your hand is being lifted in hers. 'Good boy. You're a good boy.'

Your hand is being carried till it rests against the buttons, against where she bulges. She's leaning nearer.

'Can you feel my heart beating?'

'Yes.'

'Would you like to feel it louder, just to be sure?' Her breath's coming in small gasps. She's undoing the top buttons. 'This will be our secret, remember.' Her warmth is in your hand now, her heart's fast *thud-thud*. She's making you press your hand into the bulging softness over her heart. One side, then the other, pressing your hand in deeper. You've crossed her heart and said you hope to die.

'Our secret. You can have your boat back now.' She replaced it among the scratch marks. 'Malcolm, would you like to do something for me?'

Her eyes. She's not smiling at you.

'You can really help me.' She leant forward to ruffle his hair.

They were friends now. With him, everything would be under

control, and she would be safe.

She got up from the bed:

'I want you to come with me.'

She is holding her hand out to you: 'We must be very quiet, remember, not to wake anyone up.' She ruffles your hair again, touches the side of your cheek. Placing her hand on your shoulder, she pulls you out of bed.

'A little hug first, like best of friends.' She wanted him to be near, so near. If he was with her, nothing could go wrong.

Her nightdress is still unbuttoned and you can feel her warmth against your face. She steps back.

'Come with me.' She fastened her nightdress, put her hand to her lips for silence, then led him into the corridor.

Dim light, with the carpet's softness under your bare feet.

She drew him into the room and closed the door, stood for a moment perfectly still, then switched on the bed light. The old woman's head lay on the pillow, the ornaments and scent bottles stood on the dressing table with the photographs. There would be no need for them tonight.

That same shrunken bundle of skin, bone and brittleness with her woollen bedcap over to one side. Were you going to get a row for stealing the piper?

'Mrs Goldfire's not really asleep. She never gets up any more — day and night are just the same to her. She's awake now.' She guided him over to the side of the bed. 'We'll just sit with her for a while — she's very lonely. None of her family ever visit her.'

What are you supposed to do? So long as the old woman doesn't start crying again.

'This is my nephew. Malcolm. He's sorry for the noise he was making this morning. Aren't you?'

She's turned to you and prodded your arm.

'Yes.'

'She won't answer but she hears every word you say. See how nice Malcolm is, Mrs Goldfire?' She stroked his hair. 'Such a pleasant young man. You go round and sit there, Malcolm.'

She's indicating an armchair at the other side of the bed. The old woman looks fast asleep, except for her eyes. Aunt Fiona's still talking in a kind of whisper, so maybe she's not really sure if Mrs Goldfire's listening or not. She's getting something out of a drawer. A book.

'She loves being read to. Doesn't matter where you start from — just open it and begin.' With Malcolm reading God's Word aloud, nothing could go wrong in the room. They would be in His presence, and be safe. 'You mustn't stop. Read like you did for me last night. That was perfect.'

At least it's not so heavy as the downstairs book. You begin:

'Then answered Bildad the Shuhite and said how long will ye hunt for words mark and afterwards we will speak wherefore—'

'Good boy.' She's standing in front of you, very close.

She's stroking the top of your hair.

'Wherefore—'

'You mustn't stop, remember.'

Her hand is brushing your hair back and forwards on your forehead but you aren't allowed to stop reading. 'Shall the earth be forsaken for thee and shall the rock be removed out of its place yea the light—'

'You see what a perfect young gentleman Malcolm is? Even with such lovely hair, such smooth skin, he's not distracted from God's Word. If I kiss his forehead...like *this*... he won't stop reading his Bible. If I give his ears a friendly tickle... You see. What a nice young man.'

Then she's turned away from you and gone to kneel by the edge of the bed. She's talking to the old woman but too softly for you to make out the words.

You keep reading. A couple of times you lift your eyes, but nothing seems to have changed. She's still kneeling beside the bed with the old woman's hand in hers. She's still talking. The next time you look she's holding Mrs Goldfire's hand on top of her head as if the old woman was stroking her, but was too unsteady to do it properly.

After a page you're getting tired, and cold. You read another verse, then stop. And wait.

Nothing happens. You wait another few seconds. Aunt Fiona's not talking anymore. The room is quite still now except for the old woman's breathing. Aunt Fiona hasn't said anything — maybe she's fallen asleep. Very carefully you stand up, put the Bible on the seat, tiptoe round the bed behind her, and leave.

IV

Morning

20

When Margaret came down for breakfast on Monday, the second morning back in her old house, she had found the table set for three and neither her sister nor Malcolm there. It was well after eight o'clock — was she the first up?

Most likely her sister was busy with the staff, arranging the day's work. Less fragile-looking cups, thank goodness. Not the Sunday best this time, more like Malcolm was used to. She sat down and poured herself some tea.

Through the closed door she could hear the clatter of plates as the residents' breakfasts were being prepared. There was the smell of porridge, that same damp-mealy smell that had choked every weekday morning when she was a young girl. It had sickened her then — and still did. Her mother would empty two ladlefuls onto her plate, two grey-lumpy slops:

'Eat it, it's good for you.'

The first time she'd refused, and was given nothing else to eat until some bread and milk for supper. A desperately long and hungry day, that had been. The following morning: the same *slop-slop* into her plate. Fiona, of course, dutifully ate up every last slimy spoonful — indeed, was cited as a shining example. The second day's starvation stretched far ahead into the future, one day too many.

'I'll eat it, but I don't like it,' she'd said.

'I'm not asking you to like it,' had been her mother's response. Typical.

Should she wait for the others? There was no toast in the rack.

Maybe she should go through to the kitchen to tell Daisy she was ready? Or should she make her own? This wasn't a hotel, after all.

The dining-room looked onto the garden, where it was just starting to get light. A real November morning, damp and dreich-looking. What would she do with Malcolm all day? Also, she'd have to see about getting him started at school. Heriot's? Edinburgh Academy? Their father had been at Watson's. Fiona would expect him to be sent to a private school, but they were all too far away. He was used to a five-minute walk there and back, and to having his school friends living near.

The door opened. Her sister came in, said good morning and sat down.

'Would you like some tea, Fiona?' She reached for the teapot.

Without replying, her sister immediately started talking:

'It's a raw-looking morning. Mondays seem to start earlier and last longer — I'm going to be busy all day. Mondays! And it's the end of the month with the bills and the stock checking before a trip to the Cash and Carry. Once a fortnight, you've no idea…' She paused for breath, then, as if having just noticed tea was being offered, she held out her cup:

'Thank you, Margaret. And Malcolm? Did he sleep all right in his new room? Is he settling in, do you think? Such a big change for him.' Fiona had glanced at her but looked away again before she could answer:

'A miserable, miserable looking morning. Poor Malcolm. Does he like doing jigsaws?'

'Jigsaws? Well, Fiona, I—'

'Here he is now. I'll ask him.'

Malcolm had just come into the room, still half asleep, with his hair sticking up, unbrushed. Without even giving him a chance to say good morning, her sister began:

'I was asking your mother if you liked doing jigsaws, so it's perfect timing you've appeared. Right on cue. It's such a raw-looking day outside we were wondering what you'd do as it will probably be raining soon, and then be on for the rest of the day. So do you?'

What on earth was up with her? She hadn't stopped talking since she appeared. Malcolm had glanced quickly at her sister first when he came in, then at her. He sat down at the empty place.

'Well?' Fiona leant across the table towards him. 'Do you?'

'Give him time to wake up, Fiona. Eh, sleepy-head?' Margaret smiled at him:

'Some tea?'

He nodded.

She began pouring, then turned to Fiona:

'Should I have gone through to the kitchen for toast? I wasn't sure if—'

'Toast?' Her sister made as if to get up:

'I'll see to that.'

'I don't expect to be waited on hand and foot, you know. In fact, Fiona, I was wondering what I could do to help here in the house. Perhaps if I—'

'Yes, Margaret, we can discuss all that later.' She'd turned back to Malcolm, who seemed to have fallen asleep again. 'Well?'

When he didn't respond, Fiona reached over and prodded him playfully:

'Well? *Do* you like jigsaws? If it keeps on raining we could do one this afternoon, just the two of us.'

So much for Fiona's busy Monday. In any case, Margaret was quite capable of looking after her own son. 'We'd talked about taking a look at the Castle today, hadn't we, Malcolm? The dungeons. A perfect day for it.' She half-laughed.

Finally, without looking at either of them, he raised his eyes and said:

'I don't mind.'

Her sister stood up: 'Don't worry, Malcolm.' She put her hand on his shoulder. 'We'll see you're not too fed up. If we can't do much about the weather, we can make it up in other ways. Toast?'

Margaret said:

'Yes please, Fiona.'

Malcolm nodded.

'Your mother's right: a real sleepy-head.' She gave his shoulder a quick squeeze and was just going into the kitchen when she called back:

'Brown or white?'

They both said 'white', Malcolm by giving an affirmative grunt.

Once her sister had left she looked at him for a moment. His head was back down over his empty plate.

'You're very quiet.'

'Mmm.'

'Did you sleep well in your new room?'

'Mmm. All right.'

'Well, it's morning now, so wake up. One exciting Sunday in the big city seems to have done for you.'

A long pause, followed by silence.

'Malcolm! What's up with you?'

He didn't even look at her. 'How do you mean?'

'Are you all right, son?'

Another long pause. She watched him begin turning his empty plate round on the tablecloth with his finger.

'Yes, Mum.'

'I know it's a big move here for you. For me too. With that, and everything that's happened, I know it's hard.' The table was too big to let her reach over and touch him. 'At least your aunt seems to have taken more of a shine to you.' She went over to stand beside him, but when she placed her hand on his shoulder he made no response. 'Malcolm?'

'I'm tired, Mum. That's all.' He glanced up at her:

'There's nothing wrong.'

She smiled:

'We'll have an easy day today, then. No rushing about seeing things.' She ruffled his hair, and sat down again. 'Do you really fancy doing jigsaws with your aunt?'

By way of reply the plate was turned through a second revolution.

'Hardly your style, I would have thought.'

He looked up:

'Maybe she'd let me have a go on her computer?'

The door opened. Fiona came in carrying a tray. 'Toast. Lovely fresh toast.' In an elaborate waitress-manner she placed three toast-racks on the table:

'One for my favourite nephew: Malcolm. One for my favourite little sister: Margaret. And, lastly, one for myself. Me!' She smiled and sat down.

Had her sister been at the church wine? Margaret had never seen her like this.

'Thank you, Fiona.' Then she turned to Malcolm:

'You should ask her yourself. On you go.'

He shrugged.

Fiona was looking eagerly at him. 'Shy? Come on, Malcolm. You know you can ask me whatever you want. Worst that'll happen is that I'll say no,' she laughed.

Was this woman opposite really her sister? She even looked different — livelier, younger. Overnight. A completely new Fiona.

Malcolm had woken up again:

'The Apple. The one in your office, Aunt Fiona? Could I have a go on it?'

'We'll see.' Then her sister laughed out loud:

'That's how *she* always used to answer us, wasn't it, Margaret? Our beloved mother.' Another new Fiona laugh. 'Of course you can, Malcolm. But only if I'm there to make sure nothing goes wrong.' Quickly she buttered a piece of toast. 'I'd better get a move on. No time for a leisurely breakfast this morning, I'm afraid.' Taking her plate in one hand and tea in the other, she stood up. 'Look in when you want a bite of the Apple, Malcolm.' Another laugh, and she went out.

'Will she have any games, do you think?' Malcolm asked, before starting on his breakfast.

'I doubt it. Let's hope the weather improves and we can go out somewhere.'

Malcolm shrugged and, head down, carried on with his breakfast.

It was late afternoon when Margaret came down the stairs past FEAR GOD IN LIFE, the colours of which, in the dim light, had clotted to a patch of near-darkness. Having spent most of the day sorting through the remainder of their belongings, delivered mid-morning from the cottage, she was more than ready for a break.

The noise of TV laughter came from the residents' sitting-room.

She'd looked in twice so far. Each time the scene had been exactly the same: three elderly women and one tired-looking man sitting in silence. Two of the women were in adjacent chairs, the other woman and the man each having a length of wall entirely to themselves with empty armchairs between. She'd never seen so many armchairs in one room. A cartoon had been blaring out on her first visit. When she'd looked in a couple of hours later the programme had been about dolphins: nothing else had changed. Tomorrow she might try getting to know some of the residents, but just now she needed fresh air — she'd have a walk in the garden, even if it was raining.

Five minutes later, after a damp stroll round the lawn she went up the veranda steps leading to her sister's office. Through the French windows she could see the two of them sitting with their heads close together in front of the computer. A desk light shone brightly at one side. Her sister was pointing out something on the screen, Malcolm was tapping at the keyboard. The rest of the room was unlit. She could make out the faint outlines of the filing-cabinets, the mantelpiece, the armchairs in the background. Only her sister's desk was clearly visible, isolated from the surrounding near-darkness by the work lamp and the glare of the screen.

She reached for the door handle, then paused. Her sister had indicated the top right-hand corner of the screen and said something which made Malcolm laugh. Why didn't she simply open the door and go straight in? Was she spying on them?

Fiona was typing now while Malcolm seemed unable to take his eyes from what was being written. Gradually he started to grin once more. When her sister had finished, he was sitting back, laughing loudly.

She turned the handle and went in.

Her sister looked startled. 'Margaret! I didn't know you were out there.'

Malcolm remained facing the screen.

She closed the door behind her:

'Getting on all right, you two?'

'Perfectly. But you gave me a bit of a fright: appearing out of nowhere like that.'

'I'm sorry. I hope I'm not intruding.'

'Of course not. I've just been showing Malcolm some of the custom software I use for the housekeeping programme.'

Malcolm tapped a couple of keys, but said nothing.

Custom software?

'You've taken enough of your aunt's time, I think. You'll be ready for a walk and some fresh air.'

He began getting to his feet. 'But it's raining.'

'We've got coats. Your aunt has her accounts to do and goodness knows what else. Come on, Malcolm. Let's go before it gets dark.'

'He's been no trouble, Margaret. Really.' Her sister stood up. 'A very bright boy. I'll have him running the whole house in no time!'

As Margaret turned to leave, she glanced over to see what had been so amusing about the housekeeping programme, but the screen was already blank.

Having paused at the sitting-room door to say goodnight to her sister, who was still reading in front of the fire, Margaret saw a much older-looking woman than had been with her at breakfast. Fiona was forty-seven and, this evening, looked well over fifty — as if her day's extraordinary liveliness had exhausted her. The Bible was flat on her lap, her hand flat on the page as if, too tired to keep her eyes open, she were reading the text in Braille. Had she many friends? Had there ever been a man in her life? She'd never mentioned anyone.

Margaret closed the door and began to make her way upstairs. The house was completely silent, the residents were all in bed by nine. Her footsteps were the only sound. At the second landing she stopped briefly, her hand resting on the banisters: she'd never imagined coming back here to live. For all that her mother was ten years dead, and the place run as a commercial nursing-home with safety-rails everywhere and a chair-lift on the stairs, it was the same house as always, and with the same threatening stillness at its centre.

Quietly she climbed the next flight to the top-storey landing and went along the corridor to Malcolm's room. She opened the door cautiously, and went in. There was the sound of his breathing, nothing else. He was peacefully asleep and beyond harm. She smiled to herself in the darkness, bending down to kiss him goodnight, but so carefully as not to waken him. Then she straightened up and was about to make her way to the door when she stepped awkwardly in the darkness and nearly tripped.

'Is that you, Aunt Fiona?'

Aunt Fiona? She crossed the room and switched on the main light.

'What do you mean, "Aunt Fiona"?'

No response.

'Has Aunt Fiona come to see you at night?'

Malcolm was blinking and shielding his eyes from the glare. His face was screwed up.

'Well?'

'I was asleep, Mum.'

'Has Aunt Fiona been here to see you at night?'

A long silence, then:

'Yes.'

'Malcolm. Look at me, son. I'm not angry at you.' She tried to take his hand. 'Please, I'm not angry.'

He had let his hand remain in hers, but his face was turned away.

'Listen to me, Malcolm.' She sat down on the bed beside him and leant near. 'You've done nothing wrong. It's all right, son. It's all right.'

Then she heard him begin snuffling. For several minutes she didn't speak while she stroked his hair to calm him.

What had been going on?

'There was nothing wrong,' he said at last. 'She just came and talked and… she was nice to me…'

She put her arms round him and he buried his head on her shoulder.

'Nothing wrong,' he repeated between snuffles.

'She just talked?'

'Yes.' Another snuffle. 'And she took me to see the old lady. The one I'd woken up by making a noise playing. I'd to read the Bible to her.'

'In the middle of the night?'

'I don't know when it was. I was asleep. I just read to her, then came back to bed. Nothing else.'

'Did she say she'd come tonight?'

No response.

'Better if you sleep in my room tonight. We'll take your bedding. The mattress you used when we arrived is still there.'

'What about all my stuff?'

'It'll be safe enough. Come on, son. Let's go.'

'No, it won't. Anyone could just come and take it. They could.'

Before she could say anything more he had grabbed a couple of his toys as well as his pillow. Luckily she was able to show him that the door had a Yale lock: the rest of his stuff would come to no harm.

As she went out she let it snib shut:

'That's that.'

Carrying the downie and Malcolm's clothes under her arm, she led the way downstairs to her bedroom. She would demand an explanation from Fiona in the morning.

21

Leaning against her dressing-table after pill number five, or was it number six? Had she been going back to bed?

Or had she been getting up? It was still dark. Four-three-four: red numbers on the blackest background. Four-three-four. Waiting, waiting for?

- Time to go back to bed.
- The stripped mattress, the empty room, the patterns made by the rain.
- Malcolm reaching inside the front of her nightdress, his mouth waiting to be kissed.
- Some moments of tenderness, nothing more.
- Sympathy.

Four-three-five. Feeling giddy after the last pill.

She would have to be more careful with him; make sure he didn't overstep the mark.

She wanted to be sympathetic and caring after his tragic loss.

She was so tired, and so very wide awake.

Only the faintest half-light: the top-storey corridor and landing seemed like shadows lying across darkness. Everyone was asleep, except her. Everyone was dreaming, except her. Every room was closed, every curtain pulled; every door locked. She could come and go wherever she wanted.

She, and she alone.

The whole house was *hers*.

They were all dreamers, except her. Where God commanded, nothing else mattered. Whether the sick-and-simple died today, next week or next year; whether Margaret wept or didn't; whether Malcolm received comfort or not. Set against the power of His presence, the sandstone house itself was no more solid than the residents' silly dreams. *She* looked after everything, and everyone. *She* protected them: the sick-and-simple's helplessness; Margaret's tears; Malcolm's need for tenderness.

She was going to visit her favourite nephew. As Margaret was too distressed with her own loss to give the poor boy the sympathy and tenderness he needed at this time, she herself would do all she could to comfort him. He liked her and trusted her. It was late but, as they had agreed while working on the computer, she would visit him again. He was expecting her. He would be disappointed if she didn't come.

Left-right, left-right.

Past Mrs Davidson's, Mrs Connaught's. Stumbling on the uneven carpet, nearly tripping over. Her hand finding the wall to steady herself.

Left-right, left-right.

Past Mrs Goldfire's room. Malcolm's door was next. She should turn the handle carefully to go in without waking him. That would be best: this time she wouldn't startle him. Her sudden appearance last night had upset him a little at first. She would lie down gradually on his bed, and begin stroking his hair and whispering his name till he woke. He'd be sleepy-headed but very pleased to see her. Together they would go to visit Mrs Goldfire. If he was with her, everything would remain under control. She grasped the handle and began turning it. Ever, ever so slowly. Easing it silently round.

It was stuck.

Slowly round once more, to the half turn; it stuck.

She tried again.

Again it stuck. What was wrong with it?

A moment's dizziness. She leant her forehead against the door frame, then tried again.

Stuck. Stuck.

She rattled the handle. It was locked. Malcolm's room was locked. What was he playing at?

'Malcolm?' Not too loud in case anyone heard:

'Malcolm? Let me in. It's Aunt Fiona.'

No response.

She slid back the spyhole cover but the room was in darkness. She rattled the handle again, whispering, 'Malcolm. Malcolm.'

His stupid little boy games. He *had* to hear her and come and open it. He *had* to come with her into Mrs Goldfire's room. With him she might recover God's presence. Without him…

'Malcolm!' Almost in tears now:

'Malcolm, *please?*'

Holding the handle tight. Rattling, rattling it.

Then she watched as one by one her fingers loosened their grip and let go. She was being drawn away from the door, being forced back along the corridor, further and further from God's sight. One slow step; two steps, three…

She closed Mrs Goldfire's door behind her, stood perfectly still for a moment, then switched on the bed-light. The old lady looked nothing more than a parcel of skin and bone wrapped in layer upon layer of wool blanket. Her eyes were dark smudges. The photographs were back in position and would stay there. She would never need to examine them again. The passing of days, months, years meant nothing here. She wouldn't get down on her knees, nor take the old woman's hand, nor ask forgiveness. For several seconds she stood at the side of the bed, looking down.

There was no forgiveness here.

Very faintly, far away, the downstairs grandfather clock chimed. Mrs Goldfire's eyes were closed, her hands resting on the covers. When had the old woman last heard a clock strike, and known it? Or recognized someone's voice or touch? For her, all her days must have gradually become the one same day; all her hopes and fears become so many dreams, confused into the one same dream, that shut out all the rest.

Then she heard herself say softly:

'Are you sure you don't want another pillow? A warmer bedjacket?

A cup of tea, maybe?'

The old woman did not speak.

'Shall I open the curtains a little wider? You'll see the blue sky then. You'll like that.' An encouraging smile:

'It's a lovely morning outside.' She crossed the room and pretended to open the curtains fully:

'Yes, a lovely September morning.' She could see it exactly as it had been that day ten years ago: the trees starting to turn brown, the bright sky; the Salisbury Crags so clear in the distance she could imagine reaching out to touch them. A turn, a smile and back to the bedside:

'Now, would you like me to read to you? A chapter from The Book of Ruth?' Another reassuring smile. 'I'll look after you. Don't worry. Comfortable?' That's what she had to say. Even without Malcolm she could keep God's Word in the room, and things might still be all right. She knew many passages by heart. She began:

'So she gleaned in the field until even, and beat out that she had gleaned: and it was an ephah of barley. And she took it up and went into the city…'

The window was closed, the room stifling hot. How shrunken the old woman seemed. Crumpled and huddled under the blankets: her hair flat and lifeless, her skin dried brittleness over bone, her mouth a slackness of wet muscle.

She leant over, touched the thin hair, smoothing it. She wanted to tell her everything was going to be all right; that she shouldn't cry. That she loved her.

Love. Yes, that's what she felt. Even without God she could feel love, couldn't she?

'…And her mother-in-law saw what she had gleaned: and she brought forth, and gave to her that she had reserved after she was sufficed.'

She wanted to hold her in her arms, to comfort her. Were the old woman able to speak, it would be in a whisper that was more breath than sound. She leant nearer. She was giving heart and soul trying to understand any unspoken words, and to bring comfort. Surely this was love. It had to be. With love, even in God's absence, nothing could go wrong.

Her voice faltered, but she continued:

'My daughter, shall I not seek rest for thee, that it may be well with thee?'

All she wanted was to take that frail hand, and to feel it clasp hers. Surely she wouldn't be sent away?

'And she said unto her — All that thou sayest unto me I will do.'

She lifted the near-weightless hand to her lips and kissed it. The room was growing dark around her. She must hurry. Outside, the bright September morning was rushing towards twilight. Soon darkness would surround them both. God's forgiveness always came too late.

Having leant forward to kiss the old woman's brow, she paused.

Listened. When had she stopped repeating God's Word aloud? There was a sudden silence in the room, a calmness.

She watched as her hands took one of the pillows and positioned it over the familiar face; she felt her arms tensing for the effort to come.

Her eyes were shut, her teeth were clenched, her whole weight was pressed down hard upon the pillow. There was nothing she could do to stop what was about to happen. She could hear no trace of hope in her voice crying aloud to Him:

'Help me! Help me!'

22

Something must have woken you.

It's starting to get light outside. The sound of your mother's breathing comes from her bed over by the wall.

Aunt Fiona said she was going to come to your room so you could cross each other's hearts, then go and read to the old woman again. She'll find you've been taken away. She might have come here to your mother's room to look for you, and that's what's woken you: her tapping on the door.

Maybe she's outside on the landing, waiting. If you don't get up to stop her, she'll tap louder or even start calling out your name.

So: slowly push back the downie, slide out of bed as quietly as you can.

Stand up. Wait. Listen.

Your mother's still sleeping. Feel your way past the bottom of the mattress towards the door.

The piper. Now that things have changed, with your mother bringing you down here, you'd better return the piper to Mrs Goldfire's room, or they'll think you've stolen him. You climb back onto the mattress, take him out from under your pillow, give him a slow, soundless shake to set the snow whirling again. That's him all ready for his journey back.

Cross to the door, turn the handle. Steadily, steadily, no jerking it or letting it creak.

And out, pulling it closed behind you without even a *click*.

Aunt Fiona's not there. Maybe she's gone up to the next landing to wait for you?

Listen:

No need to jump. That was just the grandfather clock chiming downstairs:

…two — three — four — five — six — seven o'clock.

Listen:

Silence. Where has your aunt gone? You must find her.

Don't turn on the stair-lights, someone might hear the snap of the switch or see them lit and come to find out what's going on. You must climb the darkness to the next floor, feeling your way up each step on your hands and knees, while keeping a tight grip of the wee piper.

Second floor. No-one's there. Your aunt's door is standing open, her room's empty.

On hands and knees again you feel your way up to the top floor, where the small table-lamp seems to make more shadow than light — as morning begins. People will probably be getting up soon so you'd better be quick. Firmly, step by step, along the corridor to the old woman's room. Her light's on. Aunt Fiona must be there already. She will be expecting you to help like before, reading aloud to Mrs Goldfire while she holds her hand. You push the door open and go in.

Aunt Fiona's kneeling at the bedside. The strap of her nightdress has slipped so it's hanging half open. She must have fallen asleep waiting for you to come. Mrs Goldfire looks awake. Her eyes are staring up at the ceiling as if she's listening out for Stella coming with her breakfast, her bedcap's tumbled to one side and so has her pillow. She's quite out of it.

This is your chance.

Quietly, the two steps over to her bedside cabinet. Lowering the piper carefully, inch at a time, down next to her lamp.

At the last moment you've rattled it noisily. She must have heard that.

Having steadied the ornament, you glance over to the old woman: she hasn't moved. Lucky. You're turning to leave—

And there's Aunt Fiona looking up at you. Her face is tear-stained, her eyes swollen and red. Without greeting you or saying she's glad you've come, she pulls her hair away from the front of her face:

'You can see that I've been crying, can't you? That I'm truly sorry?'

She looks so old, her eyes so frightened.

Before you have a chance to reply she holds out her hands:

'See? What can you *see* there?'

Is this another test?

Her hands are trembling, shaking.

'Well? What can you see?'

'Nothing. There's nothing — just hands.'

Then, slowly, she raises them to her face and begins sobbing into them. Stronger and stronger sobs that make her shoulders heave up and down. Between sobs she's repeating the same word over and over again:

'Forgive… forgive… forgive…' as if she can't finish the sentence. She seems to have forgotten you are in the room.

It's your fault that things have gone all wrong and you're much too late to read to Mrs Goldfire like last time. You have to do something. Something that will let Aunt Fiona see you still want to help her.

A moment later you've picked up the ornament again and are giving it a good shake to show the old woman how the wee piper can make snowflakes dance around him.

'Mrs Goldfire?' You shake the piper harder, holding it up for her. 'Do you like the snow?'

She doesn't turn to look.

'The snow?' Louder this time. A glance over at Aunt Fiona to encourage her as well.

Stepping nearer the side of the bed:

'The piper, Mrs Goldfire. Look at the wee piper.' Holding it up in front of her eyes now:

'You can't hear him playing his music. No-one can. But you can see him, eh?'

Should you touch her to get her attention?

'You're not asleep, Mrs Goldfire. You're just pretending, aren't you? Tell me she's just pretending, Aunt Fiona.'

There's no reply. She doesn't even seem to have heard you.

Mrs Goldfire still hasn't moved.

Getting louder:

'Wake up. You have to wake up!'

And louder. Or else, if you have to touch her on the shoulder, you know what will happen next. 'Stop pretending!' Then loud enough to deafen her:

'Wake up. Or I'll *make* you wake up.'

As if you hadn't spoken, her eyes remain staring at the ceiling. At nothing.

Then you take a step back. Lifting your arm up full-stretch.

Waiting for her to look at you, waiting for her to see you. The ornament's glass-smoothness, the wee piper's silence, balanced until the very last second in your raised hand. Then...

Full-force at the wall: *crack*. Shattering. Directly above her head.

Water dripping down; a litter of glass on the pillow, on the sheets, or her face and hair.

She keeps staring upwards. Staring...

You turn to Aunt Fiona. Her eyes are looking straight at you, but unseeing, fixed at a point somewhere far in the distance. She's breathing faster and faster.

She's leaning back, opening her mouth—

At the first sound of her scream you rush from the room, your hands over your ears. You run stumbling down the corridor — away away from that terrible noise.

Where are the stairs? You crash into the wall, scramble to your feet again with your hands still over your ears. Her screams push into your back, forcing you down the first step. The second, third...

You can't see where you are going.

Down to the next flight, your feet no longer touching the ground: Warp 2, Warp 3, Warp 4. Faster, faster than ever. Beyond the range of Mission Control.

Warp 5, Warp 6. In danger of burning up.

Warp 7—

You've come to a sudden stop at the dark window: *there's* your reflection staring at you, with the staircase and corridor curved behind. You stare back at him. He's reaching his hand towards you, and already you have extended yours across the deep window-sill to greet him in return. Once again your fingertips touch.

Your fingers press against the cold surface, and your reflection presses back. This coloured glass is all that lies between you and the small boy who stood in front of the kitchen mirror, having just found his father dead. That small boy was you, and still is — with his hand touching his reflection's.

Press harder on the stained glass. You must push further into the past, to that moment when you hesitated outside your father's door, with your hand resting on the shiny-grey paintwork.

You have started to tremble. Already you know what you are going to find in his room.

Your reflection's begun trembling, too, while it reaches further into the present, where you have just come running from Mrs Goldfire's bedside.

Your hand, your arm, your whole body is shaking uncontrollably. You must push, push your fingers as hard as you can.

Suddenly the glass begins to crack: there is the dirty-water smell of your father's bedroom.

'Dad!'

The blankness in his eyes, his stillness.

Those few seconds before you touch his shoulder have slowed down until they've lasted days and weeks, until they've brought you to this full stop: *Here.*

'Dad!'

He is falling to one side.

The crack. *Crack. Crack.*

He is dead he is dead he is dead.

You know what must happen next, what you must do:

Pulling back your arm, calling up all your strength, then screaming out loud — you smash your fist into the window.

There's blood all over your hand, and pain flowing all around you. Pain rushing into your ears. Pressing onto your eyes, your nose, your lips. If you open your mouth again, the pain will flood in, drowning you. Was this how your father died?

Is this *dying*?

You scream even louder than before.

Then stop.

Through the wrecked window come the faint sounds of Radio

One from the kitchen at the back of the house; a dog barking in the next garden, the noise of distant city traffic. You hear everything as if for the very first time.

Fiona has got up from her knees and come over to the bedroom window to wait for whatever will happen next. If she tries hard enough, she can imagine her desk downstairs covered with papers relating to the month's accounts. There, early morning sunlight will be lying like grey dust upon the carpet, the filing cabinet, her computer, the mantelpiece. Everything she needs, laid out neatly in its place. A jar of pens and pencils, sheets of paper, envelopes brown and white, stamps, a pile of bills; laundry lists, pantry lists, kitchen lists. A small digital clock, the gift of a pharmaceutical company, pulses away the seconds. Standing motionless with her back to the old woman's bed, she can picture her pen lying to hand as if she had put it down a moment ago, when she'd been interrupted by someone coming into the room; a column of figures remains incomplete. She's started crying.

Not loudly, not expressively.

If she were asked why she is crying, she would say she doesn't know. Perhaps indeed that is the very question she has been asking herself for, between sobs, she whispers the same phrase over and over again:

'I don't know, I don't know.' She wipes the tears from her cheeks as if that will stop them. Probably she would like to be downstairs in her office, working at her desk. Probably, but she really doesn't know.

She remains where she is.

Whenever she seems about to stop crying, she starts again. She has taken her handkerchief out and is biting the corner of it — to pull herself together. She has begun rocking herself backwards and forwards where she stands. Just slightly. Who could comfort her? Her sister would be sympathetic and understanding, and would try to help, but she doesn't want help, understanding or sympathy. What does she want? Is that what she is asking herself now? Repeating aloud in that same half-whisper:

'I don't know. I don't know.'

Next to a small tray containing drawing-pins, paper-clips, rubber bands and a small stapler, each in their separate compartments, there will be the plastic compass Malcolm gave her. She put it there when she last sat down at her desk. If she were there now, she might sit holding it on the flat of her hand to watch the needle tremble towards Magnetic North. That would be better than sorting through her accounts, noting them, crediting order against receipt, stock list against delivery note. Usually she never stops, not even for tea. From other parts of the house will come the sounds of vacuuming as Stella goes about her morning chores, and every so often footsteps will pass in the corridor outside; a door will open, somewhere, and close. These are what have made up the days and nights she's lived through.

She bites harder into the handkerchief, clenching her teeth until they hurt. She dabs her eyes. She begins feeling better, then without wishing to or knowing why she does it, she finds herself again repeating:

'I don't know, I don't know,' and fresh tears begin. She holds her mouth firm, refusing to whisper the words. She can feel her knuckles whitening, and senses the relief she will feel by again saying, 'I don't know…'

Then more tears bring more release. This time she is determined not to give in. She digs her nails into her palm.

The sun is rising over the Salisbury Crags. She takes several deep breaths and looks out at the garden becoming more and more visible every second: the bushes of evergreen lining the gravel path, the fruit trees, the scattering of leaves near the wall. Her finger traces out a pattern on the glass, a perfect green rectangle. The lawn. She pauses, letting her finger remain at the point where it closes the rectangle, pressing lightly onto the pane. Is *that* really her? How pale her face looks: her eyes red-rimmed, her skin's rawness showing under a smear of powder.

She can see Margaret has come to stand behind her – 'You should be in bed, Fiona' – and has remained, waiting for an answer.

'Fiona?' There's such concern in her sister's voice.

She can see fresh tears beginning to run down her face, but no sobbing, no movement. As if only her eyes were weeping and the rest of her knew nothing.

'Fiona, it's me. Margaret.'

She can see her sister's hand lying on her shoulder now. Their two reflections clear upon the window: they are not looking out at the garden, they are not speaking.

Malcolm's hand had stopped bleeding. He unclasped his fingers and there, like an unexpected miracle on his palm, was his dad's toy yacht. Had he been holding it all this time? He was certain he hadn't.

The closer his father had come to the moment of death, the tighter he would have grasped this yacht. It was time its voyage continued.

Malcolm pressed his hand down onto the broken glass littering the window-sill. More pain, but he was no longer afraid. He pressed harder until, like ice, the glass melted to a pool of clear water. He placed the boat on the surface and it floated, rising and falling on an invisible current, spreading rings of refracted colour to the water's edge. A part of the blue sky outside lay there, framed by the jagged window and the shadows filling the hall.

He breathed out gently. The small sails filled and billowed, then, almost imperceptibly at first, the boat drifted forwards. He blew a little harder, and it began to sail out towards the centre, passing between the reflected clouds like islands, and the shadows like hidden reefs. Already the toy yacht was growing smaller as it moved further away. Kneeling on the carpeted step at the edge of the small ocean, he sent fresh gusts of air until the boat was almost too small to be seen.

And all at once it was gone. He stared at the point where it had vanished, then cautiously reached out to touch the ocean.

When he turned round a moment later he saw his mother and Aunt Fiona coming down the stairs, his mother with her arm about his aunt's shoulders. Their adult unhappiness, their adult weariness were caught in the sunlight streaming through the broken window. Already he could feel the sun's warmth soothing him, like the touch of some-one's hand.

He got to his feet, and began to make his way up towards them.